ROCKY ROAD

As Frank guided the jeep partway down the mountainside, then into a gorge between two steep rock walls, he said, "Maybe we ought to look in on Ted before we—"

Frank stopped in midsentence. A loud rumbling sound was coming from overhead. The top of the jeep was off, and he glanced upward.

"What is it?" Joe said as he looked up toward where the noise came from. Then he yelled, "Frank! Watch out!"

Frank had seen it, too. Bouncing and smashing down from the bluff to their right, looking bigger by the instant, was a gigantic boulder.

It was on a collision course for the jeep!

Books in THE HARDY BOYS CASEFILES™ Series

- #1 DEAD ON TARGET
- #2 EVIL, INC.
- #3 CULT OF CRIME
- #4 THE LAZARUS PLOT
- #5 EDGE OF DESTRUCTION
- #6 THE CROWNING TERROR
- #7 DEATHGAME
- #8 SEE NO EVIL
- #9 THE GENIUS THIEVES
- #10 HOSTAGES OF HATE
- #11 BROTHER AGAINST BROTHER
- #12 PERFECT GETAWAY
- #13 THE BORGIA DAGGER
- #14 TOO MANY TRAITORS
- #15 BLOOD RELATIONS
- #16 LINE OF FIRE
- #17 THE NUMBER FILE
- #18 A KILLING IN THE MARKET
- #19 NIGHTMARE IN ANGEL CITY
- #20 WITNESS TO MURDER
- #21 STREET SPIES
- #22 DOUBLE EXPOSURE
- #23 DISASTER FOR HIRE
- #24 SCENE OF THE CRIME
- #25 THE BORDERLINE CASE
- #26 TROUBLE IN THE PIPELINE
- #27 NOWHERE TO RUN
- #28 COUNTDOWN TO TERROR
- #29 THICK AS THIEVES
- #30 THE DEADLIEST DARE
- #31 WITHOUT A TRACE
- #32 BLOOD MONEY
- #33 COLLISION COURSE
- #34 FINAL CUT
- #35 THE DEAD SEASON
- #36 RUNNING ON EMPTY
- #37 DANGER ZONE
- #38 DIPLOMATIC DECEIT
- #39 FLESH AND BLOOD
- #40 FRIGHT WAVE
- #41 HIGHWAY ROBBERY
- #42 THE LAST LAUGH
- #43 STRATEGIC MOVES
- #44 CASTLE FEAR
- #45 IN SELF-DEFENSE
- #46 FOUL PLAY
- #47 FLIGHT INTO DANGER
- #48 ROCK 'N' REVENGE
- #49 DIRTY DEEDS

Available from ARCHWAY Paperbacks

Dixon, Franklin W.

Dirty deeds

Hardy Boys Casefiles #49

This book is a work of fiction. Names, characters, places and incidents are either the product of the author's imagination or are used fictitiously. Any resemblance to actual events or locales or persons, living or dead, is entirely coincidental.

AN ARCHWAY PAPERBACK *Original*

An Archway Paperback published by
POCKET BOOKS, a division of Simon & Schuster
1230 Avenue of the Americas, New York, NY 10020

Produced by Mega-Books of New York, Inc.

ISBN: 0-671-70046-4

First Archway Paperback printing March 1991

10 9 8 7 6 5 4 3 2 1

Cover art by Brian Kotzky

Printed in the U.S.A.

IL 7+

Chapter 1

"HEY, WAIT UP!" Joe Hardy shouted, then leaned over, hands on his knees. His head was spinning. His lungs tried to suck in enough air, but they weren't accustomed to the high altitude. Unbelievable, he thought. A muscular six feet tall, Joe could run for miles when in training. But he had just sprinted one block to catch up with his brother, Frank, and he was totally winded. He brushed his blond hair off his face and panted. Squinting his blue eyes in the glare of the morning sun, he saw that his brother had stopped ahead to wait for him.

"What's up, bro? Age creeping up on you?" Frank Hardy, at eighteen a year older than Joe, studied his brother with a grin. Knowing how tough Joe was, Frank was amazed to see him now, looking as if he'd just run a marathon.

"Naw. Must be the extra muscle I'm pulling," Joe said, as he approached his brother.

Frank laughed. He, too, was feeling the effects of the mountain air. At six feet one, he had the same well-developed physique as his brother, although Frank's dark eyes and hair contrasted with Joe's coloring.

"I warned you guys—Virginia City is six thousand feet up. The air's thin, and you have to take it easy till you adjust," Kerry Prescott said, smiling at Joe. Kerry was a pretty girl of nineteen, with blue eyes and a freckled face framed by bright red hair. She wore faded jeans and a western-style shirt, which set off a slender, attractive figure. Standing with her on the wood plank sidewalk was her childhood friend, Callie Shaw. Blond-haired Callie was Frank Hardy's steady girlfriend.

"You warned us," Joe admitted, "but still, I only ran a block, and I'm ready for artificial respiration."

"We'd better take it slow for a day or two and just check out the sights," Frank said. "It's like a movie set, isn't it?"

He looked down the length of C Street, the main street in town. It was lined with Old West–style false-fronted wooden buildings that housed stores, restaurants, and saloons with swinging doors. Lined up along the raised plank sidewalks were hitching posts with a few horses tied to them. Groups of tourists drifted through town, pointing and taking pictures of the sights and of one another.

Kerry, who had lived near Callie in Bayport until the previous year, had invited her old friend and the Hardys to spend some vacation time with her in the Nevada tourist town where she was staying with her father, Ted. Callie had told Frank that Ted was an engineer, and Frank found himself wondering exactly what kind of work the man was doing.

Now, as they walked slowly along, looking into shop windows filled with wild West souvenirs, Frank said, "Kerry, why are you being so mysterious about your dad's work? Is it top secret, or what?"

Kerry stood still and looked hesitantly at her guests. Finally she said, "Well . . . okay. Do you know much about the history of Virginia City?"

"There was a lot of gold here, right?" Frank asked. "And silver?"

Kerry nodded. "This was a boomtown, the center of the Comstock lode. The mines here were the richest gold and silver producers in the world from the 1850s into the 1880s."

"Then what?" Joe asked. "They dug up all the good stuff and that was that?"

"Actually," replied Kerry, "there's still an awful lot of precious metal here, but it's buried so deep that it costs more to get it out than it's worth. At least that's what everyone thinks. Everyone except my dad, that is."

"Your father is digging for *gold?"* Callie asked with her eyes wide.

"Sssh! Keep it down," whispered Kerry, looking around. "A couple of years ago, Dad inherited a share in an old mine here, the Kingmaker. He did some research, and he thinks he knows how to get to that deep gold and silver in a way that's a lot cheaper than the old methods."

"Can he prove it?" asked Frank, intrigued.

Kerry lowered her voice some more. "He and his assistant, Mike Wood, have already *found* some gold in their tests. But Dad doesn't want anybody around here to know just yet. Not until he's certain. So keep this to yourselves, okay?"

"You can count on us," Callie answered.

"Absolutely," Frank agreed.

"For sure," Joe added. Then he looked down the street, and his eyes widened. "Hey, check this out." He tapped Frank's shoulder and pointed.

Frank followed his brother's gaze to a half dozen men in cowboy outfits, posing with some horses in front of a hitching post. The men were decked out in ten-gallon hats, leather chaps tied over their jeans, belts studded with cartridges, and huge pistols in holsters. A few held rifles, and two had long mustaches.

Frank watched, grinning, as the group glared fiercely straight ahead. A photographer squatted in front of them, snapping pictures. An older man watched from one side and rearranged the poses now and then.

"Are they for real?" Joe asked as he and the others drew closer.

"You guys got here just in time for Bonanza Days. It starts tomorrow," Kerry said. "Virginia City's biggest tourist draw. They stage shoot-outs and Old West parades, and all the local men dress up like that. Everybody's getting ready, I guess."

Joe laughed. "They look like extras for a western movie to me."

Joe noticed that the older man looked over at the teenagers when he heard him laugh. The man was tall and thin, with silvery hair. His clothes were modern but still somewhat western, including a string tie and broad white hat. "You find this amusing, son?" he called to Joe.

"Uh-oh," muttered Kerry. "Here come a lecture," she whispered. "That's Brandon Jessup. He started the Bonanza Days tradition, and he doesn't have a sense of humor about it."

Aloud she said, "Mr. Jessup, these are my friends Frank and Joe Hardy and Callie Shaw. Mr. Jessup publishes the Virginia City newspaper, owns the town's best café and the Jessup Hotel, runs the chamber of commerce practically one-handed, and—"

"And has lived in this town all his life," Jessup went on, frowning, "and knows and respects what it stands for. Do you know that Virginia City was one of Nevada's wealthiest and most powerful communities in its day? It occupies an important place in American history."

Joe nodded. "Kerry says there was a lot of gold around here."

"Yes, indeed, young man. The mines here made millionaires of a lot of prospectors who hadn't had two nickels to rub together. And the wealth of the Comstock lode turned the tide of the Civil War. This country wouldn't be the same if the gold and silver from these mountains hadn't gone to help the Union. You may find these outfits funny," he went on, waving at the posing group, "but that's the way people dressed back then. I could tell you stories. . . ."

Joe figured that the man was just getting started and tried to think of a way to turn him off. "I'm sorry I laughed," he said. "I didn't mean to—"

Jessup held up a hand and smiled. "That's all right, my boy," he said. "Actually, as much as I'm enjoying our chat, I have to get these photographs ready for the Bonanza Days edition of the paper tomorrow. But you young people can stop by my office any time, and I'll be happy to tell you about some of the—"

"Kerry! *Kerry!*" called an urgent voice. Jessup stopped, looking annoyed. Joe turned to see a young man running toward them from a car that he'd left sitting in the street, its engine still on.

"It's Mike Wood, my father's assistant," Kerry said. As he reached them, breathing hard, she added, "Mike, I don't think you've met Frank and Joe Hardy and Callie Shaw. I think you know Mr. Jessup."

Jessup gestured to the car. "Bad place to leave that, son."

Mike was small and wiry, with black hair cut short. Frank noted that the man's work pants and T-shirt were filthy and that he looked scared out of his wits.

"Is there a problem?" Frank asked.

"What is it, Mike?" Kerry demanded. "I thought you and Dad were at the mine."

He nodded and swallowed hard. "We were. I just came from there. I got here as quick as I could. I don't know what to do. Your father . . ." The assistant's eyes were wide and staring. He was having trouble finding the words.

"Slow down and take a deep breath," advised Joe. "Just say what happened."

"There's been an accident at the Kingmaker. We have this block and tackle we use to get down into the mine shaft, and Ted . . . he was going down, and the rope in the block and tackle snapped. I don't know exactly how far he was from the bottom, but . . . he fell."

"*Daddy!*" screamed Kerry. "Where is he? Is he okay?"

"He's lying at the bottom of the shaft," Mike replied. "I don't know how badly he's been hurt. When I called out to him, he didn't answer!"

Chapter 2

KERRY GASPED AND SWAYED. Joe grabbed her before she could fall.

"Are there any police nearby?" Frank demanded.

"Sheriff Calhoun's office is in the courthouse," Mike replied.

"Get over there and tell him what's happened," Frank said. "The rest of us will head out to the mine in Kerry's jeep. She can tell us how to get there. Right, Kerry?"

He looked at the girl with concern. She was leaning against Joe, an expression of shock on her face.

"Kerry?" Joe repeated gently. Callie grabbed her friend's hand.

Kerry blinked and looked around at her friends.

"I'm all right," she said faintly. "I'll be fine. Let's go."

"This is a terrible thing, just awful," Brandon Jessup remarked. "But those old mines can be dangerous places. If there's anything I can do . . ."

Frank and Joe didn't wait to hear the rest. They ran for Kerry's jeep, and moments later, they were racing out of town with Frank at the wheel. Kerry had left the top of the jeep off, and it gave Frank a wide view of the surrounding country. Kerry sat next to him, giving directions. Joe and Callie were in the back.

The road led down the mountain through desert terrain dotted with sagebrush and juniper trees. No one else spoke as Kerry directed Frank to turn onto a narrow lane of worn sandy soil that followed a cleft between two hills. Their thoughts were on Kerry's father, who was lying deep underground.

After another mile, the valley widened. Frank parked the jeep below a square opening in the side of the mountain, framed in heavy old timbers. In the wooden crosspiece at the top of the opening, someone had carved the word Kingmaker. Iron rails ran out of the mine and ended at a barrier some yards away.

As they got out of the jeep, Callie started to run toward the mine entrance. "Callie!" Frank called. "Hold it."

She turned, puzzled. "It's pitch dark in there," he explained.

"And it's dangerous," Kerry added. "Nobody's worked this mine for a hundred years. There are open shafts everywhere. Wait for us." She opened a tool kit fastened to the side of the jeep, took out two powerful flashlights, and handed one to each of the brothers.

"Right," Joe said. "We'll have to take it slow and careful. Let's stay together."

The teenagers followed the tunnel down into the side of the mountain. Joe shuddered as darkness enveloped them and the sounds of the outside world died away. The air grew cooler, and their footsteps echoed as they followed the small pool of light from their flashlights along the rails deeper into the earth. Joe noticed with relief that the walls and ceiling were braced with thick wooden beams.

"Why the tracks?" Callie asked.

"That's how they got the ore out," Joe answered. "On cars that ran on the rails. . . . Watch out!"

His flashlight revealed a pile of rocks and broken timbers blocking their way. He led the others carefully around it.

"Do you know where your father was working, Kerry?" asked Frank.

Kerry's voice was shaky. "There's a shaft a little farther in. It drops a hundred feet to a long tunnel. Dad and Mike were checking out what kind of rock the shaft walls were made of. Dad can explain, if he's—'' She stopped, not wanting to complete the thought.

They walked in silence for a few minutes until they spotted the remains of a wooden framework just ahead.

"That's it," said Kerry. "There used to be a steam-driven hoist here, but they took it out when the mine was closed, so my dad put in a little scaffold with ropes and pulleys to get up and down."

They reached the edge of the shaft, a square hole eight feet on each side that dropped into blackness. Like the tunnel, it was braced with wide beams. Fastened to the braces at the top were two heavy pulleys with thick ropes running through them. Joe played his flashlight down the length of the ropes and said, "I see a small scaffold hanging from one pulley."

Carefully approaching the rim of the shaft, Frank aimed his light straight down. "The rope from the other pulley must have broken," he said. "That's what sent Ted Prescott to the bottom."

"Do you see him?" Kerry demanded.

"I can just make out a shape at the bottom, but I can't tell how badly he's hurt. We'll need some help to get him out of there."

Kerry stepped to the edge and called out to her father. When he didn't answer after her second call, Kerry's eyes filled with tears. "What should we do?" she asked desperately.

Frank stepped back from the edge and pulled Kerry away from it. "Don't worry. Maybe the sheriff's here. He'll know what to do."

Frank led the others quickly outside. Blinking at the glare of daylight, he watched from the mine entrance as a patrol car pulled up with a squeal of tires. Mike Wood jumped out, along with a tall, thin young man in a khaki uniform. His brown hair was cut short, and his eyes were bright blue.

"Sheriff?" called Frank.

The man shook his head. "Sheriff Calhoun's out of town for a while. I'm a deputy. Name's Andy Flood."

After quick introductions all around, Joe described the situation in the shaft.

The deputy frowned. "There's an ambulance on its way from County Hospital," he said. "Let me get some rope out of my trunk, and we'll rig up some kind of—"

"You want to hitch up a safety harness," said a new voice. The Hardys turned in surprise.

Frank spotted another vehicle on the far side of Kerry's jeep. It was a battered old dark green pickup truck, piled high in the back with a strange assortment of tools, boxes, sacks, and things Frank didn't recognize. The man who had spoken had collar-length white hair and a close-trimmed white beard. He wore a blue denim work shirt, jeans, and boots with worn heels. His lined face was tanned a deep brown. He nodded to the deputy and said, "Good day, Andrew."

"Howdy, Toby," Flood answered. He turned to the others. "Folks, this is Toby Flint. He prospects for gold and silver around here. What's this about a safety harness, Toby?"

Toby walked around to the back of his pickup and rummaged in the pile until he found what he was looking for. When he brought it over, Joe saw it was a padded leather harness designed to be sat in and fastened around someone's waist.

"One of you young men can get into this, and we'll use the block and tackle to lower you down to Prescott. Ambulance ought to have something we can haul him up in. How deep is he?"

"Looks like maybe a hundred feet," Frank answered.

"Good thing he wasn't in the central shaft," Flint said, his face grim. "That one goes down a thousand feet. Well, time is wasting. Let's go."

This time Toby led the way into the mine. The others followed, armed with the deputy's long rope, Toby's harness, and additional flashlights. When the group reached the shaft, the prospector quickly hooked the harness to the block and tackle. "Who'll go down?" he asked, all business.

Frank glanced at Kerry, who stood peering anxiously down at her father's motionless body.

"I'll go," he said. He buckled the belt tightly, as Toby Flint instructed him.

"With this double pulley," Flint explained, "we can lower you real easy. Don't swing—use your legs to keep from hitting the wall of the shaft, and give us a whistle when you hit bottom. Got that?"

Frank gripped his flashlight and nodded. Then he lowered himself into the black pit. As Joe and Andy Flood paid the rope out through the rig, Frank slowly descended the rock shaft, bracing his body with his feet as he'd been told. "Wow!" he muttered as he passed Ted's scaffold and saw where the rope had parted, sending the engineer hurtling to the floor. A fall like that had to be serious, Frank thought, wondering how bad Ted's condition might be.

When he reached the bottom, Frank gave a whistle. Then he unbuckled the harness and watched it go back up.

The air felt damp and sticky against Frank's skin as he aimed his flashlight beam among the pools of standing water on the floor. He stepped closer to Ted Prescott, who was sprawled on top of a pile of canvas. Frank held his hand in front of the man's mouth. He was breathing.

"He's alive!" he called up. He heard Kerry cry out with relief. She then called down to him and said that the ambulance had arrived.

Then Joe yelled, "Coming down!" He got into

the harness and grabbed the stretcher that one of the paramedics handed to him.

Frank checked Prescott's pulse until Joe arrived a few moments later, guiding down the stretcher. "The ambulance is waiting with two paramedics," Joe informed his brother. "How does he look?"

Frank shrugged. "I don't see much blood," he replied. "His pulse seems weak, but at least he's still breathing."

Joe unfastened a long, stiff board that had been tied to the stretcher. "I convinced the paramedics that we were experienced in dealing with injuries," he said. "They'll let us bring him up. I promised to slide this board under him to protect his back before we lift him onto the stretcher."

"Right." Frank was already moving. The brothers slid the board under the limp body, carried Prescott to the stretcher, and tied him down securely. Then Joe whistled, and the engineer was slowly hoisted to the surface.

"See you up top," Joe said as he was pulled up in his turn. Frank soon followed. As he rose up the shaft, he beamed his flashlight at the broken rope.

"Whew!" Frank said when he arrived at the top to find two paramedics carrying the stretcher out of the tunnel. "Not my favorite place to hang out."

"Thanks, Frank," said Kerry tearfully as they followed the tracks back outside. "I don't know what I would have done without you guys. How can I thank you?"

"Don't worry about it." Frank exchanged a glance with Callie, who had a comforting arm around her friend's shoulders. "I think your dad will be okay."

They reached the entrance as the ambulance took off. Frank looked around, blinking in the bright light. The old pickup truck was gone.

"What happened to Toby Flint?"

"He said he had to leave," said the deputy. "He kind of pops up and disappears like that. I want to thank you boys for your help." He grinned at the boys. "I'm going to drive Kerry to County Hospital. If you'll take Toby's harness with you, I'll tell him where he can find it."

"No problem," Joe replied.

Callie offered to go with her friend, and Frank, Joe, and Mike watched the patrol car follow the ambulance.

"Well," Joe said, "might as well take Toby's stuff and get out of here."

"Not just yet," said Frank. "I'd like to go back down there for a minute."

"Back down there? Into the shaft?" Joe stared at his brother. "What for?"

"Something caught my eye. You and Mike can lower me, right?"

Mike said, "I really want to get to the hospital and look after Ted."

"It won't take long," assured Frank.

"Well, what are we waiting for?" said Joe.

A few minutes later Frank bumped his way down the shaft wall until he was level with the scaffold and the trailing broken rope.

"Hold it here," he called up. He grabbed the end of the rope and examined it closely under the beam of his flashlight, then told his brother to hoist him back up.

When he reached the surface, he took off the harness and began to coil Andy Flood's rope.

"You going to tell us what that was all about?" Joe prodded.

Frank spoke as he coiled. "When I came back up the shaft, something struck me funny about Ted's scaffold, and I wanted to take a closer look."

"Funny how?" asked Mike.

"The rope that broke," answered Frank. "The strands didn't look frayed and uneven, as if it had worn out over a period of time. It looked as if it had been cut partway through—and recently."

"Cut?" Joe frowned. "What are you thinking?"

"I'm thinking that Ted's fall wasn't an accident," Frank said. "It was sabotage."

Chapter 3

"SABOTAGE!" Joe exclaimed. "Are you sure?"

"It would take some more investigating to be sure," Frank answered. "But the strands were cut straight across, as if someone used a knife. Ted's weight was enough to break the few strands that weren't cut. We ought to do some looking around."

Joe turned to Mike. "We could use your help."

"For what?" Mike seemed puzzled.

"It looks like someone did this to Ted on purpose," Frank answered. "And you might be in danger, too. It'll help our investigation—"

"Investigation?" Mike interrupted. "You guys?"

"Believe it or not," Joe said amiably, "investigating crimes is our specialty." Joe went on to explain that he and his brother had a successful history of cracking some tough cases.

"First let's drive over to the hospital and see how Ted's doing," Frank said. "If he's able, maybe he can tell us who might have it in for him, whether anyone wants to stop what you two are doing here at the mine, if anyone else knows that you've actually found some gold . . ."

Mike's eyes narrowed. "Wait a second. How'd you know about—"

Joe interrupted. "Kerry told us. Don't worry. We can keep a secret. But the questions can wait. Let's find out about Ted."

Mike gave Frank directions as they drove Kerry's jeep to County Hospital, which was a few miles outside of Virginia City. As they searched for a parking spot, Joe eyed the low, modern building with surprise. "Impressive place for such a small town," he remarked.

"Virginia City may be small, but it's not poor," Mike explained. "Plenty of tax dollars from gold rush fortunes still support this area."

The Hardys and Mike entered the hospital and found Kerry and Callie in the lobby with Andy Flood.

"Daddy's going to make it," Kerry said, her face lit by a big smile. "They have him in the emergency room for now, but it looks pretty good. That canvas must have cushioned his fall."

"Great, Kerry!" Joe smiled back and turned to Andy Flood. "Deputy . . ."

"Make it Andy, Joe."

"Okay, Andy. Frank found something out at the mine that looks suspicious."

Andy's face grew serious as he listened to Frank tell about how the rope looked as if it had been cut.

"If someone wants Ted out of the way, they might take another shot at him once they realize he's still alive," Frank concluded.

"You'd better talk to Sheriff Calhoun about this," said Andy. "He'll be back in his office by now."

The Hardys and Mike Wood left the girls at the hospital and followed Andy to town. They dropped Mike off at his car and went to the courthouse.

Frank stepped into the sheriff's office and looked around the high-ceilinged room, glancing up at the rotating overhead fans and a bulletin board covered with notices and "wanted" posters. At a large, neat desk sat a short, stocky man of fifty years drinking a cup of coffee. He wore khaki, and his sparse black hair was combed carefully across an almost bald scalp. He was engrossed in a conversation with a woman and didn't notice the Hardys.

The woman sitting across from the sheriff had on western clothes and expensive-looking boots. She looked about twenty-five years old and had a lean face, piercing dark eyes, and shoulder-length hair just as dark. Frank noted that the flashy gold rings she wore sported genuine jewels.

"We've *posted* warning signs, but tourists wander all over," she was saying to the sheriff. "We've even found some in the mine tunnel. If anyone gets hurt, I could be sued."

"I'll look into it, Sarah, don't you worry," said the sheriff. "And let me know if there's anything else I can do for you." Then both of them noticed the newcomers.

Andy Flood introduced the Hardys to Sheriff Calhoun, explaining that they were guests of the Prescotts.

The sheriff shook hands with Frank and Joe and gestured to the woman. "This is Sarah Wright. Her family was among the founders of Virginia City. I'm sure you've noticed her house overlooking the town. It's one of the grandest of the old mansions."

Sarah said hello, and Frank spoke up quickly. "Ted Prescott's been hurt at the Kingmaker. He's in County Hospital."

Sarah's smile froze, then died. "Oh, dear," she said. "I *told* him those mines are dangerous. How bad is it?"

"The doctors say he'll make it," replied Joe. "He was working on a scaffold in a shaft, and the rope broke. He could have been killed."

The sheriff scowled and shook his head. "I

warned him. I told him those old tunnel shafts are no place for amateurs."

"The thing is," Frank broke in, "we have reason to think that his fall was no accident."

He explained his discovery of the cut rope. The sheriff listened, but he fixed Frank with a stare that was somewhat skeptical.

"Let's get this straight," he said when Frank had finished. "You think someone tried to kill Prescott, is that it? That's hard to believe. I know the folks around here, and they're good people."

Sarah Wright said, "Well, there *are* people in town who don't want the mines reopened. You remember that man who showed up here with the same idea about ten years back? I'll bet he was frightened away."

"We don't know that for sure," Calhoun replied.

"He disappeared without a trace," she insisted. "He *must* have been scared off."

"It's worth a look, isn't it?" Joe said to the sheriff. "It would only take an hour to check out what Frank found."

Calhoun looked at Joe as he considered the suggestion, but before the sheriff could answer, his office door swung open and in walked the newspaper publisher, Brandon Jessup. He saw the Hardys and nodded to them.

"What's the situation with Mr. Prescott?" Jessup asked. "Not too grave, I hope?"

"He'll be all right," Frank said.

"Those mines have seen more than their share of accidents over the years," Jessup said, looking solemn. "Back in 1884—"

"We're not sure this *was* an accident," Joe interrupted.

Jessup turned and cocked his head at Joe, examining him carefully. "*Not* an accident? What are you getting at?"

Frank stepped forward. "We think there's evidence of sabotage."

"These two green kids from who-knows-where come in here spouting a wild tale about attempted murder," the sheriff said to Jessup, "and I'm supposed to start hunting somebody down on their say-so. They've probably seen too many shoot-'em-up westerns."

"All we're saying," Frank retorted quietly, "is take a look. If we're wrong, we'll apologize for your trouble. But if we're right—"

"Sheriff, a serious charge has been made," Jessup interrupted. "A look at the mine shaft wouldn't be amiss. I'll go along to see if there's anything for the newspaper."

Calhoun hesitated, but he finally gave in. He said goodbye to Sarah Wright and drove with Jessup and Andy Flood to the Kingmaker, following Frank and Joe in the jeep.

At the mine site, Frank led the group into the mountain. "It's right down here," Frank said as they reached the shaft. The sheriff, Andy,

Jessup, and Joe gathered around Frank as he bent over and flashed his light downward.

After peering intently into the darkness, Frank stood up straight, looked at his brother, and said, "The scaffold is gone! All I can see is a length of rope hanging from a pulley."

Andy directed the beam of his flashlight straight down and said, "I think I see the scaffold lying on the floor. If we rig up that safety harness, I can take a better look."

"I'll get it," Joe offered. When he returned a moment later with Toby Flint's device, Frank and the sheriff helped lower the deputy to the bottom. Moments later Frank heard Andy call out, "Bring me back up."

When he reached the surface, his arms were full of tangled rope.

"The scaffold's down there, all right. And here's the rope it was attached to."

"Great," said Frank. "Let's take it outside in the light and have a look."

Outside, the boys, Sheriff Calhoun, and Brandon Jessup watched as Andy examined the ends of the rope. He held them up so that the others could see. The rope was old and ragged. The ends looked frayed.

"This rope sure looks as if it just gave way," Andy said, giving Frank an apologetic look.

"Right," concluded the sheriff. "And the other one must have just broken under the weight of the scaffold itself. Like I figured—an amateur who didn't know what he was doing and a couple of kids with crazy notions."

Frank took the rope from Andy. "That's not the rope I saw before," he said. "It's been switched."

Jessup shook his head sympathetically. "Frank, your light was poor, and you were swinging from that harness and made a mistake, that's all. It was clearly an accident, and that's how the paper will report it."

"Wait a minute!" Frank exclaimed.

"That's enough," the sheriff said. "You wanted us to look, and we looked. And I won't have any more wild talk, understand?"

"Rumors about murder will hurt the tourist trade," Jessup observed. "The Bonanza Days celebration starts tomorrow. We need those tourists, Frank."

Frank saw there was no point in arguing. Even Andy Flood didn't believe him. Frustrated, he and Joe said goodbye to the group and headed for the jeep to drive to the hospital.

Frank steered over the bumpy road in angry silence. Joe finally said, "If the ropes were switched—"

"There's no 'if' about it," Frank interrupted.

"Easy," protested Joe. "I believe you."

"Someone made a mistake not getting rid of the evidence right away," Frank went on. "But they took care of it later."

"Sounds like it's time to start asking questions," said Joe.

"Yup. But we'll need strong evidence to convince Sheriff Calhoun," Frank pointed out.

"Then strong evidence is what we'll get." But Joe wondered just what kind of evidence they could turn up in the tiny tourist town.

At the hospital, the brothers found Mike Wood sitting in the visitors' lounge.

"They've moved Ted from the emergency ward into a regular room," he said, looking relieved. "All signs are good."

"Where are Kerry and Callie?" asked Frank.

Mike grinned. "As soon as they heard Ted was being moved, they ran off to get some flowers. They should be right back."

"Hi, Frank, Joe," Callie called. She and Kerry came in carrying large, colorful bouquets. "Did you see the sheriff?"

"Tell you about it later," replied Frank.

"Let's go to Dad's room," urged Kerry.

They walked down the corridor, Kerry eagerly trotting ahead. Arriving first, she opened the door and darted in with her flowers.

A second later her voice rose in a shrill scream.

Joe leapt for the door and pulled it open. Ted lay unconscious in bed, an oxygen mask covering his face. His body thrashed about in convulsions, and his face was blue.

"We need a nurse, quick!" Kerry cried. "He's not breathing!"

Chapter 4

"CALLIE, FIND A NURSE!" shouted Frank.

As she raced out, Joe saw that Ted's mask was connected by a tube to a tank by the bed. He bent down and saw that the oxygen gauge pointed to Empty.

"There's nothing in that tank!" he exclaimed.

"Let's get the mask off first," said Frank.

As Kerry stared, terrified, Frank pulled at the tape that held her father's mask in place, then removed it. Ted's chest heaved as he sucked in air, and his body stopped thrashing. His face soon returned to a normal color.

"Daddy!" Kerry threw herself on her father as two nurses charged in with Callie just behind.

"What's going on here?" demanded the first nurse, pushing Kerry away from the bed. "What are you doing to this man?"

"Saving his life, we think," Joe answered. "He wasn't getting any air until we pulled that mask off."

The second nurse now looked at the small oxygen tank and gasped when she saw the gauge.

"But this was full ten minutes ago. I checked when we moved him out of the emergency room!"

The first nurse said, "The valve must have been faulty. That was quick thinking on your part," she told Joe and Frank.

The two nurses hooked the engineer to the room's built-in oxygen supply.

"Why wasn't he connected to that when we came in?" asked Joe.

"We used that portable unit to move him from the emergency ward," said one nurse. "That tank has a full hour's supply of oxygen."

"Not anymore," commented Frank dryly.

The nurse flushed. "I've never had anything like this happen before. I'll see to it that the equipment is thoroughly checked over."

When they saw that Ted was breathing regularly, the nurses left. Callie sat next to her trembling friend and put her arm around her.

Mike looked at Ted and said, "I should be going. Will he be okay?"

Frank walked out of the room with Mike and moved down the hall. "He's all right—for now. Later on we'll be asking both you and Ted about any enemies Ted might have around here. And, Mike, there's something else."

weak smile. "I just want the lunatic, whoever he is, caught once and for all."

"Poor Kerry," Callie said as they followed the exit signs to the front entrance. Out in the parking lot, she continued. "First she has to leave Bayport and all her friends, and now—"

She started to say something else, but just then Frank stopped short and nudged Joe.

"Look who's been visiting."

There was no mistaking the old green pickup truck piled with junk, or the bearded man walking toward it. It was Toby Flint.

"Andy can wait," Joe said. "Let's find out what this guy was doing here."

The prospector hadn't seen them and seemed to be in no great hurry. Then Joe called out to him. "Hey, Toby!"

Flint stopped short when his name was called, his body stiff. As Joe started toward him, the prospector took the last few yards to his truck in a few swift strides, yanked open the door, and jumped in. The ignition hesitated for a moment and then caught. Before Joe could reach it, the truck rattled off toward the exit, the boxes and tools in the back bouncing and clanging.

"The man is in a big hurry all of a sudden," commented Joe.

"And he sure has been showing up in some suspicious places lately. Let's catch him and find out why," Frank said.

The three dashed to the jeep and, with Frank driving, headed out after Toby's truck.

"He won't be able to get much speed out of that old crate," Joe remarked, buckling his seat belt. He could see the pickup a few hundred yards ahead, moving down the mountainous road toward the flat desert country, away from Virginia City.

"Where's he going?" Joe wondered out loud. "If I remember the road map, there's nothing this way until Carson City, and that's twenty miles away."

He braced himself as Frank took a sharp turn and dipped to the right. The jeep handled better than the old truck and was already eating into Toby's lead. But Toby knew the territory and where the curves were.

Frank looked at Callie in the rearview mirror to make sure she was all right.

The top of the jeep was still off, and the wind blew Callie's blond hair in all directions. Even though she was buckled in, she held on tightly to the roll bar. But she looked determined, and her eyes gleamed at the excitement of the chase.

"All right! We're gaining on him!" Joe shouted as the gap between the vehicles narrowed to less than a hundred yards. They were more than half-way down the mountain, and just as Joe decided they could overtake the pickup, the truck made a sharp turn to the left. Joe could see no road there at all.

"Where's he going?" Joe shouted above the noise of the racing engine and the wind. "That pile of junk isn't set up for off-road— Wait a minute. There's a trail there!"

Sure enough, Frank spotted two parallel tracks, overgrown with brush, heading away from the road. He slowed for the turn and switched the jeep into four-wheel drive. The heavy-duty tires bit into the dirt track, and the jeep lurched ahead. Both truck and jeep threw up huge clouds of dust in their wake.

"I think he made a mistake, going off the road," Joe yelled. "We're better equipped for this kind of—whoa, watch out!"

The jeep sailed off a little hill, and all four wheels left the ground for a moment. It landed with a jarring thump. Frank looked back at Callie and asked, "How are you doing back there?"

She laughed. "It's just like a roller coaster! Good thing I have my seat belt on."

"Look," said Joe. "He's turning right."

Frank instantly followed, slamming into potholes and running over clumps of sagebrush.

Callie leaned forward and shouted in Frank's ear, "Does he know where he's going?"

"I think so," Frank yelled back. "It looks like there's something up ahead."

Out on the horizon Joe saw a thin green line. Toby seemed to be heading straight for it. As they got closer, the line took shape as a thick tangle of trees and bushes. Joe blinked at the sight of such a vivid green, compared to the sandy colors they had been racing through.

"What is that?" he asked. "Some kind of water hole?"

But Frank didn't take the time to answer. Toby's pickup was speeding up again. The jeep was a hundred yards back.

"He's got more power under that hood than I figured," said Frank. He watched as the old pickup reached the edge of the trees, made another sharp right turn—and disappeared.

Frank put his foot to the floor and followed the truck into the trees. Suddenly the trail hooked to the right and dipped into a steep gully.

Toby Flint, knowing the terrain, had slowed down to make the dangerous blind curve. Frank had not. Realizing that he was moving too fast to stay on the track, Frank braked and shifted to a lower gear. The jeep shuddered, and its engine howled.

"Frank!" Callie screamed.

For a second Frank thought he had made the turn safely, but then a rock appeared in front of the jeep, too big to ride over and too close to avoid. Frank's reflexes took over, and he slammed on the brakes with all his strength and turned the wheel.

There was time for a quick flash of worry about Callie before Frank's head crashed into the steering wheel. Then he felt an instant of blinding pain, and everything went black.

Chapter 5

"FRANK?"

Frank awoke and blinked his eyes. His head hurt, and there was something wrong with his sense of up and down. He shook his head in an effort to clear it. A wave of greater pain told him that was a mistake. He relaxed and closed his eyes until the pain eased and he could remember what had happened. Then, carefully, he tried opening them again.

The jeep was lying on its right side, and Frank was still in it, leaning sideways in his fastened seat belt. Other than his head, nothing hurt, which was encouraging.

"Frank?" Joe bent forward to look at his brother's face. "You okay? Can you hear me?"

"I can hear you," Frank croaked. "I don't know if I'm okay. Get me out of this thing."

With Joe's help, Frank freed himself from the seat belt and climbed out of the jeep. Taking a few tentative steps, he was relieved to see that all parts were still in working order. "What happened?" Frank asked his brother.

"The jeep tipped over when you swerved to avoid that rock. Luckily, you were going slow enough for Callie and me to brace ourselves when we pitched over."

"Callie!" Frank suddenly called out, grabbing Joe's arm.

Joe pointed in front of the overturned vehicle. Callie was lying on the ground, but her eyes were open and she was conscious. Kneeling by her side and examining a scrape on one arm was Toby Flint. His old truck stood a little farther down the trail.

"What's he doing?" Frank demanded.

Joe grinned and shook his head. "When he saw us skid off the trail, he slammed on his brakes and came speeding back to help."

The prospector looked up. "It's not serious," he said. "She's lost a little skin, but it just has to be cleaned up and bandaged. Don't you know any better than to hot-rod around like that when you don't know where you're going?"

"Don't *you* know any better than to take off like a scared rabbit when somebody calls your name?" asked Frank. He felt sore and grouchy.

"What're you talking about? I drove home, that's all."

"Oh, right." Frank was annoyed. "You had that old heap of yours revved up as high as it would go. I'm surprised it's still in one piece. Why did you run like that?"

Toby looked offended. "It's not an old heap. And the reason I tried to avoid you, if you want to know, is because I don't like getting mixed up with the law, the way you seem to be. The sheriff already thinks I'm a good-for-nothin' bum. He'd love an excuse to give me grief."

"What were you doing at the hospital?" Joe demanded.

"I was asking after Prescott," said Toby. "Guess he'll pull through."

"We need to ask you some more questions," Joe insisted.

Toby waved him off. "First let's get that jeep right side up. Then we can tend to the young lady."

He backed his truck up and, after tossing some boxes out, revealed a power winch bolted to the bed of his pickup. With the Hardys' help, the jeep was soon hooked up and righted. Frank was relieved to see that it had suffered only dents and scrapes. Toby replaced the boxes in the back of his truck.

"Follow me," he called.

"Where?" asked Frank, helping Callie up.

"This is my neighborhood you're in. Let's go."

Joe looked around. There was no sign of civilization to be seen. He stared at Toby. "You call this a neighborhood?" he asked.

"Come on," Toby insisted.

Joe shook his head and joined Frank and Callie in the jeep. It started up immediately, and they followed Toby's truck as it wound down through the trees until they found themselves on a riverbank. Sure enough, there stood a rickety shack thrown together with pieces of unmatched scrap lumber. A stovepipe stuck through the roof and a rocking chair sat in front. Near the chair, grazing on some weeds, stood a mule.

"Will wonders never cease," Joe said.

"Where are we?" asked Callie as she got out of the jeep.

Toby waved his hand outward. "That's the Carson River," he explained. "This here"—he pointed to the mule—"is Beulah. I sometimes take her out prospecting instead of driving the truck. And this is home."

Toby led the way into the shack. Inside, it was filled with cast-off furniture, but everything was clean and, Joe noticed, somehow pleasant. There was a shelf full of worn books over a desk. While Toby bustled around, Frank looked the books over. They were mostly concerned with mining, geology, metallurgy, and mechanics.

Toby produced a first aid kit and soon had Callie expertly bandaged. Then he sat down on a low stool and sighed.

"I suppose you won't give me any peace until I talk to you. So go ahead. Start your questions."

"How come you're so interested in Ted Prescott?" asked Frank. "What is he to you?"

"I don't have any particular interest in him," Toby insisted. "I was worried about him, that's all."

"You were nearby when he fell down that shaft," Joe pointed out. "And when he was almost killed in the hospital, there you were again."

Toby sat up straighter. "Almost killed in the hospital? How?"

Joe raised his eyebrows skeptically at this reaction. But he explained about the faulty oxygen tank.

Toby scratched his head. "Well, I didn't have anything to do with either. But *someone* wants him dead, it looks like."

"Any ideas who?" Frank asked.

Toby thought for a moment. "There are people in Virginia City who are suspicious of anyone who wasn't born here. And there are some who say they hope the mines never start up again in a big way, because they like the town quiet, as it is now, and mining would mean more people and noise and smoke and dirt." Toby paused.

"Then there's a lady named Sarah Wright."

"We met her," Joe said.

"She's a friend of the sheriff. She likes to think she's the queen of the Comstock lode," said Toby. "She had a run-in with Prescott because she believes her family owns the Kingmaker mine outright."

"Any chance she's right?" Frank asked.

Toby shrugged. "The way they used to stake claims in those days, who knows? You'd write your claim on a scrap of paper, stick it in an old tobacco can, and leave it on a marker, which could be anything, maybe a pile of stones. Here, take a look."

He rummaged through a drawer in an ancient rolltop desk and pulled out a folder. From it he took a yellowed sheet of paper that had been laminated in clear plastic.

Frank took it and read out loud.

" 'Notice is hereby given that the undersigned locates and claims the following piece of mineral-bearing ground as a lode claim: From this marker, five hundred feet in a northerly direction, eight hundred feet in a southerly direction, and three hundred feet on either side.' "

Frank looked up. "The claim is dated April 1877."

Toby nodded. "That's a genuine claim. Eventually it would get registered, but it was valid from the moment it was left there. You can see how there might be problems with a setup like that. Sometimes claims overlapped, and there were arguments, even shoot-outs. All those veins of gold and silver ore interconnect below the surface, so the claims were never exact. A miner could run a tunnel into someone else's pay dirt, and claims got jumped if someone had a mind to steal. It was pretty wild back then."

"Where'd you get this?" asked Frank, studying the paper.

"Found it, out there somewhere." Toby waved a hand. "Can I have it back now?"

Once Frank had returned the paper, Toby went on. "Anyway, Ted had a big shouting match on C Street one day with Sarah and that Don Douglas."

"Don Douglas?" asked Joe.

Toby made a sour face. "Sarah Wright's fiancé. He's a local fellow, got a mean, vicious temper. I hear he used to get in lots of fights when he was a kid, and he still talks nasty. He threatened Ted, warned him that the Kingmaker was off limits."

"Is that a fact?" Frank said, looking over at Joe. "We'll file that away. Anyone else?"

"Well . . . it seems to me that Sheriff Calhoun doesn't like Prescott much. But that may be a case of the old-timer not trusting the newcomer—I can't be sure. Other than that, like I say, some locals may not like what Ted's doing, but that doesn't mean that they'd kill him to stop it. There's one person I'm certain has nothing to do with it."

"Who?" Joe demanded.

"Me," Toby replied, standing up. "Will that do?"

"For now," answered Frank. "We'll be on

our way. Come out and get your harness. It's in the jeep. And thanks for the help with the jeep and the first aid."

Toby nodded, unsmiling. "It's nothing. Would've done the same for anybody." He followed them outside and took the harness from Frank.

Callie and Joe thanked Toby and got in the jeep.

As they drove back toward Virginia City, Frank shook his head thoughtfully. "I don't know. Toby doesn't seem like a killer to me. Did you see how surprised he looked when we told him about the oxygen tank business?"

"It could have been an act," Joe pointed out. "You have to admit he is one strange guy, living out in that shack, no electricity, no company. I think he knows more than he's talking about. He also likes to avoid the sheriff."

"That's true," Frank agreed. "But his secrets might not have anything to do with what happened to Ted. I'd like to check through the back-issue files of the newspaper, if we can."

"What for?" asked Joe.

"Sarah Wright mentioned something about another man trying to start the mines up a while back and then disappearing. I'd like to see what we can find out about that."

Callie leaned forward. "Let's stop at the hospital and pick up Kerry first."

At the hospital they found that Mike Wood had joined Kerry again. Ted was sleeping.

"He woke up for a minute," said Kerry. "He recognized me and smiled. Then he fell asleep."

"That's good news," said Joe. "We're going to town to look through old newspaper files," said Joe. "Want to come?"

Kerry hesitated, glancing at her father.

"Go ahead," urged Mike. "I'll stay here with Ted for now."

Kerry gave him a grateful smile.

"Okay, but first let's drive back to the house," she said. "I want to get some things for Dad before it gets dark."

"Uh, Kerry, we have some other news," Joe said as she left with the Hardys and Callie. "It's about your jeep."

Kerry looked puzzled as they stepped out into the parking lot. Then she stopped short and frowned at the sight of the battered jeep, which was covered with a layer of dust. Joe told her what had happened with Toby Flint.

"Do you see Flint very often?" he asked after Frank apologized for the state of the jeep. "Does he hang around your father much?"

Kerry shook her head. "Oh, I see him sometimes, in that rolling junkyard of his, or with that mule. I always think he's on his way to look for gold or something. Anyway, I've never given him much thought. Why?"

"We're just collecting information," Frank told her. "You never know what'll prove useful."

Joe watched the house the Prescotts had rented appear over a low rise a mile from town. A prefab outbuilding stood alongside. Ted had converted it into his laboratory and office. As soon as the jeep rolled up in front of the house, Kerry jumped out.

"I'll just be a couple of minutes," she said. "You can wait out here if you want."

"Wait a second," called Joe, whose gaze had caught something in the other building. "Kerry, does your father leave his lab door open?"

"No, he always makes a point of locking it. He's very careful about the papers and things in the office. Why?"

"Because," said Joe, "the door is open now."

Kerry gasped and started toward it.

"Kerry, wait up!" Frank called. "Let's go together. Just in case someone's still in there."

As they approached, Joe saw that the heavy padlock was dangling loose and that the edge of the door showed signs of having been forced with a pry bar. Slowly and carefully, he swung it fully open.

Kerry let out a soft cry.

The large room was a shambles of scattered paper and overturned furniture. Broken glass was scattered everywhere.

"Someone has broken in and ransacked the place!" Joe exclaimed.

Chapter 6

"OH, NO," Kerry said softly. "All of Dad's work . . . all of his equipment." She knelt down to pick up a folder from the floor.

"Wait, Kerry," said Joe, putting a hand on her shoulder. "Don't touch anything until the sheriff's people have a chance to go over the place for fingerprints. We'd better call him right away. Where's the phone?"

"Over on that table." Kerry pointed to it. Joe saw that its wire had been ripped from the wall.

"I'll use the phone in the house," said Frank, going to the door. He stopped and looked back at Joe. "At least Calhoun can't call *this* an accident."

Frank walked outside and approached the front door of the house, but as he reached for the knob, he froze.

He could hear someone moving around inside.

Quietly, carefully, Frank turned the doorknob and let himself in. He looked to the left of the entryway into a den, where a desk stood under a window. A man was standing at the desk with his back to Frank, leafing through some papers.

"Find what you're after?" Frank asked.

The man spun around, startled. He was big, a couple of inches taller than Frank, and in his mid-twenties. His jeans and tight-fitting shirt showed off the kind of muscles acquired during long sessions in a gym. The expression in his black, deep-set eyes was not guilty as much as angry.

"Who are *you?*" he asked, putting the papers down and crossing his arms. His manner was designed to intimidate, but Frank looked back calmly.

"I'm someone who has a right to be here," he replied. "What's your story?"

The man said, "I don't know you. You must be another stranger to this town, like Prescott. I'm Don Douglas, and I don't like strangers all that much."

"Well, I'm Frank Hardy, and I don't like people who break and enter."

"Watch your mouth, kid. The door wasn't locked, so I didn't break in."

"Is that so?" Frank asked. "What about the lab? Is the sheriff going to believe you when he finds your fingerprints all over in there?"

At the mention of the sheriff, Douglas looked a little nervous. "Now, look," he said. "That lab was just like it is now when I arrived. I had nothing to do with the mess. I admit I took the chance to look around some, but I'm no vandal."

Frank kept his eyes on the other man. "How did you get here? I don't see a car."

"I walked. It's only a mile or so from my house, and I like the exercise. Listen, I'm getting tired of this questioning."

"You might have to get used to it," Frank said. "Why are you so curious about Ted?"

Douglas took a quick step forward, and Frank tensed. But Douglas stopped and smacked a large right fist into his open left hand.

"Because he doesn't belong in this town!" he shouted. "There are people here who have rights that go back a hundred years. Prescott can't waltz in and steal people's property out from under their noses. I won't let him get away with it!" He started to step around Frank.

Frank stood firmly in his path, and retorted, "How do you plan to stop him?"

"I've had enough of this," Douglas said. "Get out of my way."

Frank didn't budge. "I think you'd better stick around until the sheriff gets here."

"You're messing with the wrong man, punk," growled Douglas. He grabbed Frank's shoulder tightly with his large right hand.

Frank knocked the hand away with a whiplike

motion of his left arm. "Don't rush off," he said, adjusting his stance in case Douglas charged him. "You'll have to talk to Calhoun sooner or later."

Douglas's face turned red, and he brought up his fists. He went into a boxer's crouch, though Frank saw that he wasn't trained at it.

Stepping in, Douglas let go a roundhouse right. Frank bent backward to allow it to sail by, then dug a left hook into the bigger man's midsection. Douglas made a wheezing sound and stepped back, surprised. Frank figured that it had been a long while since anyone had stood up to the man.

Then Douglas began to cautiously circle around Frank, feinting punches but not throwing any. Frank held his ground, pivoting as Douglas jabbed and glowered.

Abruptly, Douglas came forward and brought his right leg up like a man punting a football, hoping to catch Frank with the pointed toe of his fancy cowboy boot.

But his reflexes and speed were no match for Frank, who swiftly sidestepped, grabbed Douglas's foot and, placing his own leg behind the man's ankle, toppled him over backward.

Douglas landed hard and scrambled back and away. Reaching up to the desk, he grabbed a metal paperweight and fired it hard, aiming for Frank's head. Frank ducked, and the paperweight smashed a framed picture on the wall behind him.

Each failure made the dark-haired man angrier. He bellowed and charged at Frank, butting him with his head and grabbing him around the waist. Frank took Douglas's head in both hands and then clipped him in the jaw with his knee. Douglas thudded to the floor, made a weak attempt to raise himself, and finally collapsed.

Half an hour later, Frank sat in the den trying to fit together the broken pieces of the picture frame while Calhoun, Andy Flood, and two other deputies dusted for fingerprints and took notes. Sheriff Calhoun had already taken statements from the Hardys, Callie, and a very distraught Kerry. Don Douglas sat quietly with a swollen lip, glaring at Frank.

"*Now* are you convinced?" Joe asked the surly sheriff.

"It sure does look—" Andy Flood began, but Calhoun's voice rode over the deputy's.

"So someone has a grudge against Ted Prescott. That's no surprise. His plans for the mines might not sit well with a lot of people. But all I see is a case of breaking and entering. I *don't* see anything that points to attempted murder."

Joe rolled his eyes in frustration.

"What makes you two such experts, anyway?" the sheriff asked.

"Our father was a cop for years," Frank

answered. "We learned a lot from him." He explained that Fenton Hardy, after his police career in New York City, had become a private detective and built a reputation as one of the best.

The sheriff shook his head. "A *city* cop from the East. No wonder you two see killers behind every bush. But out here it's different. The people here are decent. You don't understand that, do you?"

"Can you believe this guy?" Joe muttered.

Frank spoke quickly. "Sheriff, we're not saying the whole town is full of murderers, just that there may be one man who is very dangerous."

The sheriff stood up. "Well, I don't see it like you do, and I'm still the law around here."

"What are you going to do about *him?*" Joe asked, pointing to Don Douglas. "Or is he just another honest citizen?"

"I'm taking him in with me," said Calhoun. "And he'll be charged, don't you worry. The deputies will be finished in the lab in a while, and then you can clean up in there."

He turned to Kerry. "I'm sorry about your problems, young lady. Come on, Andy."

The young deputy looked troubled. But he took Douglas by the arm and started out after his boss.

As they got to the door, Douglas stopped and turned to face Frank. "You and your brother should keep to yourselves. The people of this town don't like strangers coming in and meddling. This is a warning."

"Let's go, Douglas," said Andy, and yanked him outside.

"Remember what I'm telling you," Douglas said.

Frank looked out the window, watching the sheriff drive away, and saw that the sun had set. "It's too late to go to the newspaper office," he said. "It'll keep till morning."

Kerry telephoned the hospital and got Mike Wood. He said that Ted was resting comfortably and that he had arranged for a cot to be brought into the room so that he could spend the night there. Kerry thanked Mike and hung up. "Mike's staying with my father, and Dad seems to be okay. I didn't tell them about the break-in. I don't want my father to get worried right now."

"I don't blame you, Kerry," Joe said. "Maybe Douglas will confess, and then your father won't have anything to worry about. But I have my doubts. Tell me, do you think the sheriff could be involved in what's happening? It's hard to believe that he won't investigate the case just out of stubbornness or stupidity."

"I don't like him," Kerry said. "He's not doing his job, if you ask me."

"No, he isn't," Frank agreed. "But if, as Toby said, Sarah Wright has such influence around this county, the sheriff might only be following her lead. They seem to be friends. And we know what Ms. Wright's motive would be—she thinks the Kingmaker is hers."

"What about Toby? Maybe he tore up the lab," said Joe.

"He could have," Frank responded. "He had the opportunity, as far as we know. And he had the means. I just don't see that he had any motive, do you?"

"None that we know of," Joe admitted. "But he said he's avoiding the law. Maybe he's jealous of Ted. I mean, here he is, wandering around the desert looking for a few nuggets of gold, and along comes Ted Prescott with part ownership of a whole mine."

"That doesn't sound like much of a motive," Frank said.

"Maybe not for most people. But most people wouldn't want to live in a shack in the middle of nowhere, with no one for company but a mule. That kind of life would make a guy crazy after—how many years do you think he's been there? Did he say?"

"Let's find out how long he's been living there tomorrow," Frank said. "Maybe Jessup can tell us when we go to the newspaper office. He seems to know everything around here."

Joe groaned. "If we ask him about Toby Flint, he'll want to tell us about the history of every prospector who ever came through Virginia City. The guy is a wind machine."

Frank grinned. "Try not to look too bored when we talk to him. Someone with his knowledge of this area can be helpful. We should also talk to Andy. He seems to be a reasonable guy."

Frank turned to Kerry. "Why don't we clean up the lab and get some dinner?"

"Let's just close it up for now," Kerry said. "I'm too tired and hungry to do anything but eat and go to sleep."

They all went out with Kerry to lock the lab, then returned to the kitchen and made some sandwiches. After eating, Frank and Joe said good night and went to the guest bedroom they shared. It wasn't late, but they were tired and quickly fell asleep.

Hours later, Joe woke suddenly with a sense that something was wrong. The luminous dial of his watch read three o'clock. He wondered what could have woken him in the middle of the night. Then, out of the corner of his eye, he saw something move on the bed.

A full moon cast its silvery light through the window and reflected off something long and thin with a glossy surface.

Joe's eyes grew wide as he saw what it was. He was sharing his bed with a five-foot-long diamondback rattlesnake.

Chapter 7

FIGHTING AN IMPULSE to yell, Joe froze. Any sudden move, he knew, would frighten the snake. Forcing himself to remain still, he whispered to his brother, in the other bed.

"Frank! *Frank!*"

Frank woke instantly, hearing the urgency in his brother's voice. He followed his lead, keeping his own voice low. "Something wrong?"

Joe lay like a statue, watching the snake slither slowly up the bed. So far, the creature had not been alarmed.

"There's a snake—a diamondback rattler, I think—crawling up my bed."

"Okay. Stay calm, and *don't move*."

"Right. Thanks for the tip," Joe said, as he fought his urge to run screaming from the bed. He didn't like snakes. "Any other brilliant ideas?"

"As soon as I get one," Frank whispered back, "you'll be the first to hear it."

Keeping his own movement and noise to a minimum, Frank sat up and searched the room for something he could use to capture the snake. Between the beds was a heavy Navajo rug with a colorful geometric pattern. Moving with care, he reached down, lifted one end of the rug, and gripped it in both hands. "Joe? When I tell you, roll off the bed toward the wall. Got that?"

"Got it."

The snake suddenly sensed Joe's presence. It whipped its body into a coil, and Joe heard the frightening clatter of the rattles in its tail.

Frank, *hurry up!* Joe thought, but he didn't dare speak.

"Now!" Frank ordered.

As Joe hit the floor, Frank jumped out of his bed and dropped the bulky rug over the snake before it could launch itself in a strike. He quickly rolled the rattler up inside the rug, which was too thick for its fangs to penetrate. The muscular snake tried to thrash its way free, but Frank wrapped the rug in the blanket from Joe's bed.

Joe stood and took a deep breath. He looked at the bundle on the bed, which twitched and shifted around.

"If it's all the same to whoever brought this," he said, turning on the lights, "I'd rather have a dog."

The bedroom door opened, and Callie peered

in. "What's going on in here? Kerry and I heard a thump. Did someone fall out of bed?"

The two girls came into the room. Frank told them about the snake.

Callie looked pale. "Someone's trying to kill *you* now," she said to the Hardys.

Frank shook his head. "I don't think so. It must have been meant as a warning. Even if the snake had bitten Joe, it probably wouldn't have killed him."

Joe's laugh was a little shaky. "That's very comforting," he said.

"It was more likely a threat," Frank decided.

"But who did it?" Callie persisted.

"Well, who knows we're helping Ted?" asked Joe. "There's a pretty long list. Sarah Wright, Don Douglas, Toby Flint. Even Calhoun and his deputies, plus any number of others who might have heard about us from them. And no one's going to have an alibi for three in the morning."

"I'd bet on Don Douglas," Frank said, thinking about their last confrontation. "But let's put it on hold for the time being. I vote that we call it a night and try to get some more sleep."

He picked the wrapped-up snake off Joe's bed. "I'll just drop our friend outside first."

After leaving Kerry at the hospital the next morning, the Hardys and Callie went to the newspaper office. Brandon Jessup agreed to let them look through the back issues, which he had stored on microfilm.

"Mr. Jessup, do you know Toby Flint?" asked Joe.

"Just to say hello to," the silver-haired man replied. "He's a throwback, you know, to when the Comstock mining started. Those prospectors panning for gold were brave men who faced many hardships. There was one colorful fellow who—"

"Mr. Jessup," Frank interrupted, "has Flint ever actually found any gold?"

"He's never struck it rich, but he comes in with small nuggets and dust occasionally. I'd say he manages to make barely enough to meet his living expenses, such as they are."

"What about Don Douglas?" Joe asked.

Jessup smiled. "You two are lucky to find an old man like me who loves to talk. Douglas was a terror around here as a youngster. I remember a lot of people were sure he'd come to a bad end. But he's settled down, and now he's engaged to Sarah Wright. I'm sure that she's a good influence on him. She's from a wealthy Virginia City family, you know."

Frank cleared his throat. "We'd better get at those files. Thanks for letting us go through them."

"My pleasure," Jessup said. "The history of a colorful city is in those back issues. If you have the time, read through the early decades.

You'll find out all about Virginia City's glory days, when it was—"

"We'll try to do that," Joe assured him.

"Well," said Jessup, "the Bonanza Days festivities are about to start, so I'll leave you to it."

The brothers sat at microfilm viewers and started going through the spools of film, each one containing a year's worth of newspapers. Callie read with Frank.

After they'd been reading for an hour, it was Joe who called out, "I think I've found something."

Frank and Callie stood and read over Joe's shoulder. The article was in an issue of the paper printed ten years before. It told of a young engineer, Jonas Middleton, who had just arrived in town. He planned to test a method that he hoped would restore the Comstock mines to full productivity.

The article quoted him. " 'There is still a huge amount of wealth buried in those hills. Until now, the cost of getting to it has been too high to justify the attempt. But my method will change that.' "

Joe scrolled ahead, looking for further mention of Middleton, but there was none for a few months. Then Frank spotted a small paragraph buried deep in the paper, headlined "Man Missing."

The article stated briefly that Jonas Middleton

was believed to be missing after failing to keep several appointments in Virginia City in one week. There was no indication in the story about whether Middleton had had any results with his mine experiments.

"Does that tell you anything?" asked Callie.

"Only that, as Sarah Wright was saying, there may have been people in Virginia City ten years back who didn't like the idea of anyone getting gold or silver out of the mines," Frank said. "They may have driven Middleton away."

"Could they be the same people who want Ted out of the way?" asked Joe.

"If not the same ones," replied Frank, "then at least people with the same reasons."

They left the office and started down C Street. Virginia City's main avenue was bustling with shoppers and sightseers. As they walked past a saloon that looked as if it had been preserved in time, they heard gunshots ring out.

"What's going on?" Callie asked.

Joe saw tourists crowding around where the shots had come from. "Let's check it out."

Joe saw that a mock gunfight was in progress between local citizens dressed in old-time western outfits, who shot .45s loaded with blanks. One of them, wearing a sheriff's badge, fired up at a gunslinger in a black hat who stood on a balcony over the saloon. The man clutched his chest and toppled off the balcony, landing on a wagon full of hay.

"That wasn't bad!" Joe said as the tourists applauded.

Just then Frank grabbed Joe's arm and pointed to the other side of the crowd. There, watching the action and laughing, were Sarah Wright and Don Douglas. Douglas's laughter stopped as he saw the Hardys. He looked as if he wanted to confront them, but Sarah managed to pull him away.

"He wasn't in custody very long," Joe said, staring after them. "And look, the sheriff is with him."

As the crowd of tourists broke up, the brothers and Callie watched Sheriff Calhoun walking down the sidewalk on the other side of the street, Don Douglas and Sarah Wright going in the opposite direction. In honor of Bonanza Days, Calhoun wore a glittering red, white, and blue get-up with leather chaps and, on his boots, stirrups that clanked.

"Does he have any idea how funny he looks?" Callie asked as they crossed the street.

"Not a chance," Frank replied, lowering his voice as they got within earshot.

"Morning, Sheriff," Frank said with a straight face. "Nice outfit."

"I had it made special," Calhoun replied.

"What's the story on Don Douglas?" asked Joe. "We saw him on the street just now."

"I let him out on bail. But don't worry, kids.

I chewed him out pretty good before I let him go."

"That's all? You chewed him out and let him go?" Joe couldn't believe it. "Did you slap his wrist, too?"

The sheriff scowled. "Hold on, there! Don't you tell me how to do my job. The man oughtn't to have walked into someone's house uninvited, but that's all he did. He didn't steal anything. We have no proof that he did anything else illegal. There's nothing to connect him with the damage to Prescott's laboratory."

Callie gasped. Joe started to say something more, but Frank tapped his brother on the shoulder and said quietly, "Let's go."

"Why didn't you tell him about the rattlesnake?" Callie asked as they walked back to the jeep.

"What for?" Joe replied. "He'd have said it was just a harmless joke by another law-abiding citizen."

"Let's get out of here," Frank suggested. "I want to call Dad."

"What for?" asked Callie.

"If he knows a good investigator around here, we can get some background on Don Douglas."

"Good idea," Joe said. "And on Toby Flint and Sheriff Calhoun, too."

As Frank guided the jeep partway down the mountainside, then into a gorge between two steep rock walls, he said, "Maybe we ought to look in on Ted before we—"

Frank stopped in midsentence. A loud rumbling sound was coming from overhead. The top of the jeep was still off, and he glanced upward.

"What is it?" Joe said as he looked up, toward where the noise came from. Then he yelled, "Frank! Watch out!"

Frank had seen it, too. Bouncing and smashing down from the bluff to their right, looking bigger by the instant, was a gigantic boulder.

It was on a collision course for the jeep!

Chapter 8

FRANK QUICKLY REALIZED that he couldn't stop the jeep in time. There was no room to swerve either left or right. So he floored the gas pedal, and the jeep leapt forward. The ground shook as the boulder hit the road five yards behind them.

"Look!" screamed Callie, staring up. Another giant rock was rolling down in front of them. Frank slammed on the brakes just as the boulder landed with a jarring crash, inches from the jeep's front fender.

A voice rang out from overhead. "We could've killed you just now. We can kill you whenever we want. Get out of Virginia City!"

Joe frowned. "Friendly place, isn't it?" He squinted up at the top of the rock wall. "I'm going to look around up there."

"Is that such a great idea?" Frank asked as Joe climbed out of the jeep and studied the cliff. "They might have guns."

"If they had guns," replied Joe, "they would've used them by now." He started up the steep rise, using crevices and the tough plants growing out of the rock for handholds. They were lucky for one thing, Frank thought as he watched his brother. Joe was a skilled rock climber.

"Did you recognize that voice?" Callie asked Frank as they got out of the jeep.

"Nope. I'm pretty sure it was a man, but that's all I could tell."

Ten minutes later, Joe scrambled back down. He dusted himself off and caught his breath.

"They're gone. Oh well, I needed the workout. All I can tell you is that they wore boots."

"Great! Fantastic clue." Frank laughed. "That narrows the suspects down to half the population of Virginia City and the surrounding territory."

Joe shrugged and glanced over Frank's shoulder. He saw Toby Flint and Beulah, who had a load of tools on her back, coming around a bend.

"Look who's here, right where the action is, as usual!" Joe said as Toby walked around the boulder that blocked the jeep and joined them.

"Morning," Toby said. "What happened here?"

"Maybe *you* could tell *us*." Joe stared at the bearded man suspiciously.

Toby looked at both boulders. He looked up at the top of the bluffs. "I'd guess that somebody isn't feeling very friendly toward you people."

"We figured that out. Do you know anything more about it?" Joe asked.

"Me? Just what I see," said Toby. "Beulah and I are on our way to the Bonanza Days parade."

He gestured to the boulder in front of the jeep. "I can give you a hand moving that smaller rock."

From the gear on Beulah's back, he produced two long pry bars and gave one to each brother.

"You two put your weight on those bars, and I think you can move that to the side of the road."

Frank and Joe were able to muscle the rock out of the way in a few minutes.

As Toby replaced his tools, he looked at Joe. "You seem to have me pegged as a bad guy. You're barking up the wrong tree, young man. I don't want to hurt anybody."

"Thanks for the help," Joe said, not commenting on Toby's statement.

"It's all right. You kids seem to need a lot of it. You'd better look sharp, because I may not be nearby next time you need a hand."

"Maybe you will, and maybe you won't," Joe said, but so softly that only Frank heard him.

"I'll tell the sheriff about this monster rock here," said Toby. "They may have to blast it into smaller pieces to get rid of it. Want me to tell Calhoun the rock was meant for you?"

"Don't bother," said Joe. "He'd just say that we were in a falling rock zone and that accidents happen."

Toby and his mule resumed their walk into town as Frank aimed the jeep toward the hospital.

"I know," Frank said, anticipating what Joe was about to say. "Toby Flint could have done it."

Joe nodded. "Those pry bars he had—Toby could have used them to roll the boulders down at us."

"Do you think he's strong enough to do that?" Callie asked.

"Don't let the white hair fool you," said Joe. "He's tough enough."

In Ted Prescott's hospital room, Callie and the Hardys were pleased to find the engineer awake and chatting with his daughter.

"The doctor says that I can go home if I promise to rest up for several days," Ted said with a big grin. "I want to thank you, Frank and Joe, for all your help." The grin faded. "I understand my lab is a disaster area."

"I think Don Douglas is mixed up in what's been happening to you," Frank said, pulling up a chair. "Joe's more suspicious of Toby Flint."

"Flint?" Ted considered the possibility. "He does keep tabs on me. He might envy me my mine, but I don't think he'd get violent."

"What can you tell us about Sarah Wright?" Frank asked.

"Sarah Wright thinks she owns all the mineral rights around here because her family's been here forever. She wanted to hire me to work for her—provided I recognize her claim title to the Kingmaker. I told her my claim was approved by a court of law and that I was working for myself.

"That set her fiancé, Douglas, off. He's greedy and a bully. I wouldn't have thought he'd have the guts to try to kill me, but a whiff of gold might have given him the nerve."

Frank told the Prescotts about the article on Jonas Middleton and his unexplained disappearance.

"I know that name!" exclaimed Ted. "I think he actually may have rented the house Kerry and I are living in now. While we were moving in I found a hidden compartment in the desk that was left in the study. There were papers inside, including a rental agreement signed by Middleton. As a matter of fact, I used that hiding place to stash my important records. At least whoever trashed the place didn't get them."

Joe noticed a folded cot leaning against a wall. "Mike slept here last night?"

"Right," Ted replied. "And Kerry relieved him this morning. He's gone out to the Kingmaker to salvage some things that were left in the shaft in all the confusion yesterday."

"How long has he been working for you? What's his story?" Frank asked.

"I met Mike in California," Ted said. "He's from Ukiah. He doesn't like to talk about his past—I think he had a rough childhood. I was working on a tunnel up there. Mike was just an errand boy for the crew. But he was smart and I liked him, so I made him a sort of apprentice. He's been with me ever since."

Ted frowned. "Wait a minute. You're not suspicious of *Mike*, are you?"

"That's silly," Kerry said. "Mike would never harm my father."

"We're not accusing him of anything," Frank assured the Prescotts. "We're just learning everything we can, and then we'll see what has bearing on the case. Which reminds me, can we use your telephone to call our father in Bayport?"

"Be my guest," replied Ted.

Frank reached his father at home.

"How's the wild West?" Fenton asked.

"Wilder than we expected. We've gotten mixed up in a case, and we could use some help."

"I might have known," Fenton replied. "What can I do for you?"

"We need someone local to run checks on possible suspects. Do you have a contact?"

"Hmm. Wesley Dunne is a good man in Reno. That close enough? He owes me a favor."

Frank wrote down Dunne's phone number and, after filling his father in briefly on the status of the case, hung up and called the man in Reno.

"You're Fenton Hardy's son?" Dunne had a pronounced western drawl. "Well, then, whatever you want, just say the word."

"We need to find out anything we can about some people," Frank said, "especially if they have criminal records."

"Give me the names and a way to reach you."

Frank spelled out the names Sarah Wright, Don Douglas, and Toby Flint and gave Dunne their approximate ages.

"Ask him what he knows about Sheriff Calhoun," Joe prompted.

Frank did so, and then added, "One last name for you—Mike Wood, from Ukiah, California. He's about thirty."

"I'll get right on it," Dunne said.

"Why Mike?" Kerry asked after Frank had thanked the man and hung up.

"Only because he had the opportunity to commit most of these crimes," Frank said.

"But he wouldn't!" she replied forcefully.

"It's just a formality," Joe assured her.

"I'd like you kids to do something for me," Ted said. "Would you carry a message into town?"

"Sure thing," Joe agreed.

"I'd like you to find Sarah Wright and Don Douglas. They're sure to be there for the Bonanza Days parade. Tell them that if my system works, there's going to be enough gold and silver to make us all rich. I'm willing to cut a deal with them. I'd like this craziness to end, right now."

"They may have tried to kill you," Joe said. "If they're the guilty ones, they should be nailed."

Ted's jaw was set. "Nobody's dead yet, and I don't want any more violence. My mind's made up."

Frank saw that Ted was determined. "Okay," he said. "We'll go right now."

"I'll stay here with Kerry," Callie decided. "She looks like she could use some cheering up."

On the way into town, Frank said to his brother, "This doesn't mean we have to stop our investigation. And Sarah and Don might not be the ones we're looking for."

"You're right. Maybe Ted's deal will stop Don or Sarah and buy us some time to prove one of them is guilty—that is, if it is one of them.

"Looks like the parade's in progress," Joe observed. As he searched the crowd for Sarah and Don, he saw a group of horseback riders trot by in the wake of a high school band. Brandon Jessup was among them, riding a beautiful glossy black horse. He waved to the Hardys as he rode past.

But Joe was distracted by a precision drill team riding by on small dirt bikes, wearing the badges and hats of a fraternal organization. Next, a truck towed a flatbed trailer carrying the hulk of a rusty old airplane. The brothers laughed at a sign that proclaimed it to be the Virginia City Air Force.

It was a relief when there was a momentary lull in the parade. In the silence, a salvo of gunfire was heard.

"Uh-oh," Joe whispered. "Here goes another shoot-out."

He pointed to a man who had just burst out of the local bank, wearing an old-fashioned high-collared shirt and, on his head, a green visor.

"Help! Help!" the man yelled. "They're robbing the bank! It's Black Bart and his gang!"

Joe laughed as the crowd lining the street whispered excitedly and several video cameras focused on a group of horses tethered to a hitching post in front of the building.

Sure enough, a group of men charged out of the bank and leapt on the horses. They wore flashy western clothes and had bandannas tied over their faces. The men waved big revolvers, which they fired into the air.

"They must go through dozens of cases of blank cartridges here," Frank said, smiling.

He watched as two of the men, who were wearing badges, started blazing away at the "bandits," who fired back and galloped toward where the Hardys stood. The air smelled strongly of gunpowder.

As they raced by, one of the masked men fired his pistol at the brothers. Frank felt something hum past his head, and behind him the wood shingle on the corner of a building splintered.

"That was no blank!" Frank shouted to Joe over the noise of the gunplay and the excited crowd. "Someone's shooting real bullets!"

Chapter 9

THE MASKED RIDERS pulled their horses up at the edge of town, where the parade route had ended. But a single horseman galloped on, headed for open country.

Frank saw that the members of the drill team had parked their dirt bikes at the end of the street. "Come on!" he yelled to Joe.

They sprinted toward the bikes. Frank went up to one of the drill team members. He was an elderly man who wore wire-rimmed glasses and had white hair sticking out from under his hat.

"Can we use a couple of these bikes for a minute?" Frank asked. "It's an emergency."

The man stared. "What kind of emergency?"

"Life and death," Frank said. Another man overheard and came over.

"Aw, go ahead, Walt," he said to his friend. "These two look all right to me. You bring them back, hear?"

Frank and Joe kicked the bikes to life and roared off. The lone horseman had disappeared over a ridge, but the Hardys spotted him in the distance when they reached the top. They speeded up, but the rider dismounted and ran to a car parked at the side of the road. The car sped away, raising a cloud of dust, which made it impossible for the Hardys to get a clear look at it.

The abandoned horse, its reins dangling, stood quietly grazing on a clump of weeds.

Frustrated, Frank and Joe rode the bikes back to town, where they returned them to the owners.

"Take care of your emergency?" asked the one called Walt.

"Not quite, but thanks anyway," Joe said.

Frank went up to the men dressed as bank robbers, who were standing in a group with their horses. "Did any of you get a look at the guy who rode on when you stopped here?"

They gave him blank looks.

"What guy?" asked one. "It was all happening so fast, I didn't notice."

"Oh, yeah," said another. "One fellow kept right on going. I figured he must've had pressing business somewhere."

Frank spotted Andy Flood nearby and called him over. "Where's the sheriff?" he asked.

"Over by the museum, last I saw him," replied Andy. "What's up?"

"A guy who was riding with the bank robbers shot at me as they came by," explained Frank. "He had live ammunition. We chased him, but he got away in a car, and we couldn't get a good look at it. Oh, and he left the horse he used standing about a mile out of town."

"You'd better find the sheriff," Andy said. "I'll see to the horse."

Calhoun was easy to locate in his showy outfit. His smile vanished when he saw Frank and Joe running up. "What is it now?" he asked, scowling.

"We've been shot at," Frank said. He told the sheriff about the extra bank robber.

"You have any witnesses?" he asked Frank. "Aside from your brother, that is?"

"There was too much noise and excitement. I don't think anyone saw. But I know the sound of a bullet going by, and it hit the wall behind me. I can show you where."

Calhoun followed the brothers to where they had been standing. Frank pointed to the spot where the bullet had chipped the wooden shingle.

"You call that *evidence?*" asked Calhoun.

"He felt something going past his head, too," Joe said, feeling his anger rise. "He could have been killed!"

Calhoun bent down and picked up a small blob

of plastic. There were many of them scattered on the ground. He held it out to the Hardys.

"Wadding," he explained. "They pack it in blank cartridges, and sometimes it shoots out almost like a bullet, except it can't really hurt you. That's what you must have felt going by."

"Unbelievable!" Joe exclaimed, unable to keep his fury in any longer. "What kind of law officer are you, anyway? You won't look at facts when they're staring you in the face."

Frank put a hand on his brother's shoulder. "Calm down," he said.

Now it was Calhoun's turn to explode. A small crowd gathered to watch.

"You two are a pair of troublemakers if I ever saw any! I've got half a mind—"

"That's a generous estimate," Joe snapped.

"*Enough!* One more word, *just one,* and I'll toss you in jail for disturbing the peace. Now get out of my sight!"

Frank thought he'd have to haul Joe away bodily, but his brother saw that Calhoun's threat was real, and he walked away willingly, though his jaw muscles remained clenched tight.

Suddenly Sarah Wright and Don Douglas stood facing the Hardys. Sarah looked disapproving, and Don smirked.

"You guys aren't so popular here just now, are you?" Don asked them.

"Where were you twenty minutes ago, Douglas?" asked Frank.

"Right on C Street, watching the parade, if it's any of your business."

"I'll vouch for that," Sarah added. "He's been with me since the parade began. I'll swear to it, if I have to."

"You won't have to," Joe answered. "We have a message for you, from Ted Prescott."

"Has he finally decided to be reasonable?" Sarah inquired. "Everyone knows that my family has a right to whatever ore is still in that mine. They paid for it with their blood and sweat."

"Ted wants to work out a deal that'll make everyone happy," Frank said. "He says he'll forget what's happened up to now."

Sarah and Don exchanged a look.

"We have an appointment now that we can't break," Don said. "You two come out to Sarah's house at three this afternoon, and we'll have an offer ready for Prescott."

After giving the Hardys directions to her house, Sarah strolled away arm in arm with Don. The Hardys watched them go, then realized that Toby Flint was standing a few feet away and must have heard the conversation. The white-haired prospector waved.

"Still in one piece, I see," he said. "That's good to know. Well, I'd better get Beulah home. She gets grouchy if she isn't fed on time."

"What is it with him?" Frank wondered. "He shows up everywhere."

As Frank and his brother drove the jeep back to the hospital, Joe asked, "Think we ought to tell the Prescotts about getting shot at?"

"Ted has enough on his mind as it is," Frank said. "I don't see the point in it."

They stopped at a pay phone in the hospital's lobby to call Wesley Dunne, the Reno investigator.

His nasal drawl greeted Frank on the other end. "Got a few items for you," he said, "but not much. That Don Douglas has a few busts for disturbing the peace, and he was on probation for an assault. That was all several years ago."

Dunne continued. "Sarah Wright is an upright citizen. I haven't found anything on Toby Flint, and I'm waiting for word from Ukiah on Mike Wood. And your Sheriff Calhoun is tough and runs his territory the way the local big shots want it run—peaceful and quiet. But there's nothing to suggest he's corrupt. Anything else?"

Frank felt disappointed. He'd hoped for a more definite clue. "Not right now, Mr. Dunne," he answered.

"Fenton Hardy's son can call me Wesley. I'll let you know what I hear from Ukiah."

Frank hung up, and he and Joe went to Ted's room. The engineer was sitting up, chatting with Kerry and Callie.

"I can leave here this afternoon," he said when he saw the Hardys. "Did you see Sarah Wright?"

"Frank and I have an appointment to meet her and Don at her house later this afternoon," said Joe. "They're willing to talk, at least."

"Good." Ted sighed and leaned back. "Maybe we can put this nightmare behind us and get back to work."

"I hope you're right," Frank said. "Of course, you realize that someone other than Sarah and Don may be behind your trouble."

"Even if that's true," Ted replied, "it'll be a good thing to get along with those two. Life here will be easier with local people in my corner."

"I'm starving," Frank announced, "and hospital food has never agreed with me. Callie, Kerry, want to get lunch with us?"

"I think we'll stay here with Ted," Callie replied. "We're having fun talking about when we were in grade school together."

"There's food at home," Kerry said. "Just help yourself to whatever's there."

"Thanks. We'll see you after we go out to Sarah Wright's place," Frank said.

Frank and Joe stopped at the Prescott's for some lunch and continued on to Sarah Wright's house.

As the jeep pulled up in front of the mansion, Joe gave a low whistle. The house stood on a street above town with a few other old mansions, but it alone had been kept in beautiful condition. Huge and newly painted, the house was trimmed with ornate carvings. Several of the windows were ornamented with stained glass, and a broad porch filled with rattan furniture ran the width of the house.

"Kerry's dad said Sarah's great-grandfather built this at the height of Virginia City's boom years," said Joe.

"Looks like business sure was booming," Frank commented.

The front door had an antique doorbell with a key that had to be twisted. Joe did so, and they heard the bell inside. But nobody answered the ring. He tried again, with the same result.

Frank knocked and, under his fist, the heavy door swung slightly open.

"Ms. Wright?" he called. "It's Frank and Joe Hardy. Anybody home?"

There was no response.

He pushed the door farther, and they looked inside. The room was furnished with antique furniture and decorative pieces that were as old as the house itself. It looked like a display in a historical museum—except it was a total wreck.

Two huge sofas had been upended. The glass on a framed photo on one wall was shattered, and the shards lay all around. Several pillows had been slashed, and their stuffing was lying about in heaps. Tables were upended, and one delicate end table had a leg broken off.

"Maybe whoever did this was after Sarah Wright or Don Douglas," suggested Joe. "They could be lying hurt somewhere."

"Maybe," replied Frank, feeling both doubt and suspicion.

"We'd better call the sheriff right now," Joe said.

A siren wailed outside, got closer, and died away as a patrol car pulled up in front.

"It looks like someone called him for us." Frank went to the front door and looked outside.

Then the realization dawned on him. He punched the door frame in frustrated anger. "We've been set up!" he exclaimed. "Look. None of the antiques have been ruined. Just some pillows and the glass."

Joe's mouth dropped open. But it was too late to do anything.

Sheriff Calhoun swaggered inside with his revolver drawn. Behind him came Andy Flood.

"Well, look who we have here!" the sheriff boomed, with a broad smile on his face. "You two troublemakers have finally crossed over the line."

He turned to the deputy. "Andy, cuff them!"

Chapter 10

"GREAT ENDING to a perfect day," Joe grumbled, exchanging a weary look with his brother as Andy Flood snapped the handcuffs on his wrists. Sheriff Calhoun, still in his sparkling Bonanza Days regalia, stood by looking smug, revolver in hand.

"Now check the house, Andy," he ordered. "I'll guard these two."

Andy gave the handcuffed Hardys an unhappy look and did as he had been told.

"We had an appointment here," Frank said. "Sarah Wright asked us to come over."

"Uh-huh," said Calhoun, clearly enjoying the turn of events. "Did she tell you to demolish her house, too?"

"You were tipped by an anonymous phone call, right?" Joe asked.

"It's not for you to ask," the sheriff retorted.

The deputy returned. "The back door was forced open," he said.

"The way I figure it," said Calhoun, holstering his gun, "you wrecked this place to pressure Ms. Wright so she'd give in to Ted Prescott. Maybe Prescott even suggested it. No proof of that, of course," he said regretfully.

"Even you can't really believe that," Frank said. "This was a setup, Calhoun. Don't you see that nothing of value in this house has been destroyed? And anyway, we got here just a few minutes before you did."

"Got any witnesses?" asked Andy Flood.

"Afraid not," answered Joe. "After we left the hospital, we went to Ted Prescott's house to eat lunch, and then we came here."

"I'll handle this, Andy," growled the sheriff.

"What about fingerprints?" demanded Joe. "We don't have gloves."

"That's an easy one," Calhoun replied. "You wrapped towels or pillowcases around your hands."

"Give it up," Frank said to his brother. "The man wants to take us in, and that's that."

"First sensible thing you've said," Calhoun commented.

He loaded the Hardys into the patrol car and had Andy follow in the jeep. At the courthouse, he led them into his office for booking.

"Andy, you go find Sarah Wright and ask her

if she had an appointment with these two. We'll do it by the book."

"Want to bet on what she'll say?" Joe asked his brother.

Frank said nothing.

As Andy Flood left, Brandon Jessup walked in.

"Anything good for the paper, Sheriff?"

"We caught a couple of vandals," replied Calhoun. "These two were up at Sarah Wright's house, smashing everything in sight."

Jessup looked sternly at the Hardys. "I'm sorry to hear that," he said. "I didn't think you guys were that kind."

The booking procedures—mug shots, fingerprints, and forms—had just been completed when Andy came into the office with Sarah and Don. The sheriff stood respectfully.

"I'm sorry to bother you, Sarah, but we found these two up in your house in the middle of a real mess. There's a lot of damage, I'm afraid."

Sarah gasped. "Oh, no!"

"They claim that you had arranged to meet them there," Calhoun continued. "That true?"

"Certainly not," she replied, glaring at Frank and Joe.

"But they did talk to us today, after the parade," Don Douglas said. "They threatened us—well, Sarah, actually. They said she'd be sorry for making things hard on Ted Prescott."

Joe let out a humorless laugh.

Calhoun shot a nasty look at him, and then turned back to Sarah and Don. "Thanks for your time. We needn't trouble you further. You two, come with me," he said to the brothers.

He led them back to the section that had served as the town jail for many years. Joe eyed the dark cells and saw that the walls were covered with fifty years' worth of graffiti. Two cots with thin mattresses sat against the walls. Frank and Joe entered, and the sheriff slammed the heavy door.

"Make yourselves comfortable, fellows," said Calhoun. Then he turned away and walked out.

"Well, I guess we made his day," Joe said.

Joe sat on the edge of one cot, and Frank stretched out on the other. He could feel the springs through the mattress, and the gray blanket on top was scratchy. There was no pillow.

"What I want to know," Frank said, "is why Sarah Wright and Don Douglas did this."

"You think they're responsible for everything else that happened?" Joe asked.

"We know they have a motive," Frank replied. "About means and opportunity, I don't think we've got a good case. I'm almost certain Don Douglas couldn't have been the masked horseman who shot at me, for instance. We saw him in town right after it happened. So if they are the ones behind it, they had help."

"And it wasn't Toby Flint, either," mused Joe. "He was in town, too, when we returned from chasing the rider. Though I still don't put him completely in the clear. Just because we haven't found a motive for him yet doesn't mean he doesn't have one."

Andy Flood came to the door of the cell and looked in. "How are you guys doing?" he asked. "Want something to eat?"

"Not now, thanks," Joe said. "A little conversation would be nice, though. We've been meaning to talk to you."

"Andy, why is Calhoun coming down on us so hard? Why does he refuse to even consider the possibility that someone is trying to kill Ted Prescott?" asked Frank, sitting up on the cot.

Andy flushed and thought for a moment. "I shouldn't be talking to you like this," he said. "But my instincts tell me that you're not criminals. You have to understand that Calhoun has been sheriff here for twelve years. He likes it. And it's an elected position."

Andy paused and looked toward the door to the sheriff's office, making sure no one could hear. Then he continued.

"If important people around town, like Sarah Wright, decide they'd rather have someone else wearing that badge, why, that's what will happen. So he won't go against them, not unless one of them is found holding a smoking gun. Ted Prescott's a newcomer. He doesn't carry any weight here. Neither do you two."

"Did you hear that phone call—the anonymous tip?" asked Joe.

"I answered it," Andy said.

"Anything unusual about the voice?" Joe asked.

Andy's brow wrinkled. "Nope. It was a man, but I didn't recognize the voice."

Frank stood up. "Could you do us a favor?"

Andy looked uncomfortable with the idea. "I don't know if I . . ."

"It's no big deal, nothing illegal," Frank assured him. "Just let Callie Shaw, my girlfriend, know what's happened to us. She's either at the hospital or at the Prescotts' house."

Andy hesitated.

"The fact is, we *are* entitled to a phone call, and we didn't get it," Frank pointed out.

"I guess that's true. All right, I'll do it." Andy headed out of the office.

Twenty minutes later, Callie was facing them through the bars of the cell.

"Hi, guys. Sorry I didn't have the time to bake a cake with a file in it," she said. "Kerry dropped me off. She had to get back to her dad. What happened?"

Frank told her about what they had found at the Wright mansion and that the sheriff had showed up.

"Ted is back home," Callie said. "He'll be in a wheelchair for a couple of days. Oh, and I have a message for you from that detective in Reno."

"Wesley Dunne," said Frank. "What's he say?"

"He said that he hasn't been able to find a trace of Toby Flint before he arrived in Virginia City. Also, he heard from Ukiah. There is nobody named Mike or Michael Wood who fits the facts that you gave him. His conclusion is that both of them are using assumed identities for some reason. But"—Callie hesitated—"I can't imagine there'd be anything wrong with Mike."

Joe stood up. "I had a hunch that Toby Flint had something to hide. But I didn't figure on Mike Wood."

"Don't jump to conclusions about him," Frank cautioned. "There may be a simple explanation. Maybe he isn't from Ukiah but from some tiny village nearby. Or maybe Michael is his middle name and he decided to use that because he hates his first name. But it raises some interesting possibilities."

"Like what?" Callie asked.

"We can deal with them later," Frank said. "Right now we've got to get out of here. When you get back to the Prescotts', try to find Dad as quick as possible. Tell him we're in jail, and it's vital that we get out right away."

Callie nodded. "Anything else?"

"As long as we're here, you and Kerry have a big job on your hands."

"What do you mean?" Callie looked worried.

It was Joe who answered her. "We were set up so that we'd be out of the way. And the sheriff won't be of any use, because he doesn't believe, or doesn't *want* to believe, that Ted Prescott is in danger."

"You're making me nervous," Callie said.

"Good," Frank replied. "You *should* be nervous. Now that we can't protect Ted, there's a very good chance that whoever's after him will try to kill him again."

Callie turned pale. She swallowed nervously and said, "But what can we do?"

"Does Ted keep any weapons at home?" asked Joe.

"I think Kerry said something about a rifle," Callie answered.

"Find it and make sure it's ready to use," said Frank.

"Also," Joe added, "no one should go outside once it gets dark. Draw all the curtains and don't stand in front of a lighted window. Make sure the doors are locked."

"Wow," whispered Callie. "If you're trying to scare me, you're doing a great job!"

"Maybe nothing will happen," Frank said, "but you'll be ready if it does. The main thing is to get Dad busy on springing us out of here."

"What about the deputy?" Callie asked. "Maybe he could help protect us."

"We'll talk to Andy," said Joe. "But my guess is that he has strict orders where we're concerned."

"I'd better be going," said Callie. "I'll drive the jeep back." Her eyes met Frank's through the bars. "See you soon—I hope." She gave him a kiss through the bars and squeezed his hand.

"Count on it," he said. "And call us every few hours. Andy'll take the messages."

"Okay," she said, turning to leave.

After she left, Frank began to pace the cell. Joe watched his brother and began to grow restless himself.

"Why don't you try to relax?" Joe suggested.

Frank ignored him. "I *hate* this," he growled. "Callie and the others are under the gun, and we're cooped up here because Calhoun is too worried about keeping his job to do it right."

He slammed a hand into a bar. "If something happens to Callie . . . to any of them, while we're sitting in here, I'll . . ."

He couldn't finish. Joe had never seen his brother so worked up.

"Hey, don't drive yourself crazy. Callie's tough. She can take care of herself."

Frank said nothing, but he started to pace again, like a panther in a cage.

Slowly it grew dark. Frank stopped pacing and

threw himself full length on his cot. Silently he stared up at the ceiling.

When footsteps sounded in the corridor half an hour later, he sat upright. It was Andy Flood.

"Your girlfriend called," he told Frank. "She said to tell you both that your father wasn't available, but she's left messages for him. Also that they've done everything you told them to do."

"Thanks, Andy," Joe replied. "Listen, is there any chance we could talk to Sheriff Calhoun again? Maybe we can get him to at least patrol near the Prescotts' house."

"Not until tomorrow. He had to go up to Tonopah on business and won't get back until morning."

"That's just great," Frank growled, and dropped on his bunk again.

"Hey, don't bite my head off. I've got orders to follow." Andy sounded hurt.

"Don't take it personally," Joe said. "He's just worried about Callie and the others."

Andy nodded. "I wish I could help. But there's nothing I can do. My hands are tied."

"Sure, I know," Joe answered.

After Andy left, time crept by, and now and then Joe would try to start a conversation.

"Dad's sure to have gotten the message by now. We'll be out in no time."

But Frank said nothing.

Joe decided to take another shot at getting through to Frank. "Listen, bro, things may not be all that bad. We could be overreacting, imagining—"

"Not that bad?" Frank sat up and fixed Joe with a steely look. "Overreacting? Callie could be standing between Ted Prescott and a murderer. She could take a bullet meant for him." Frank began to pace the room again.

Joe saw that it was useless to try to calm his brother down—being confined to a cell was getting to both of them. After another ten minutes Joe drifted into sleep. His brother's voice woke him.

"Joe! Joe!"

"What is it?"

"It's after midnight, and we haven't heard from Callie since eight o'clock."

"What can we do?" Joe asked.

"We can call them," Frank said. "Andy! Hey, Andy!"

"Be right there," called the deputy.

"What's the problem?" Andy asked, appearing at the cell door.

"Listen," Frank said. "Could you call the Prescotts' number and make sure they're all okay out there?"

Andy squinted at his watch. "At this hour?"

"They're expecting to hear from us. We don't want to keep them waiting." Frank's voice took on a pleading tone that Joe hadn't heard before. "Please? Just a phone call."

"Oh, I guess so," Andy replied, and went to

the office. Frank stood at the cell door and waited for his return. Andy was back a moment later.

"Sorry, Frank, there's some kind of problem with the lines. I couldn't reach them."

Frank's knuckles whitened on the bars. "Couldn't reach them?"

"No dial tone, no busy signal, nothing. I guess the line is down. I'll call the phone company in the morning."

"Andy, don't you understand?" Frank yelled. "The problem with the line is that someone's cut it! They're being stalked by a killer!"

Chapter 11

THE DEPUTY STEPPED BACK. "Come on, Frank, cut it out! We don't know what—"

Frank cut him off. *"I* know! Joe and I have known all along. Someone wants Ted Prescott dead, and he'll take Kerry and Callie down, too, if they're in the way. We have to get out there, *now!"*

"That's crazy talk, Frank," the deputy said. "Relax and get some sleep. I'm on duty alone tonight, my orders are to stay here, and that's what I'm going to do." He walked quickly away and slammed the door to the office.

Frank watched him leave and whipped around to face Joe. "I'm not going to sit here while Callie and the Prescotts are in danger. No way!"

"What do you have in mind?" Joe asked, not liking the look on Frank's face.

"I'm getting out of here," said Frank.

"But how?"

"Any way I can. Are you with me?"

"Frank, breaking out of jail is a felony. You're asking for major trouble."

Frank nodded, staring at his brother. "I *have* to do it, Joe. I have to help Callie. Look, if you don't want to get involved, I'll understand. But I couldn't live with myself if Callie or any of the others met up with a murderer."

Joe stood silent, thinking for a long time, before he came to a decision.

"Okay, Frank. It's your call. What do you want to do?"

"Get Andy back here. Tell him you have a headache or something, that you need aspirin. I'll be lying on my cot. Try to get him close enough to the bars so we can grab him."

"I *like* Andy," Joe said with a sigh. "He's a nice guy. I hate to do this to him."

Frank looked at Joe and said, "So do I. But we don't have a choice." He lay on the cot as Joe called out.

"Andy! Hey, Deputy!"

"What is it now?" Andy yelled through the closed door.

"You have any aspirin out there?"

"Just a second," Andy shouted.

The door opened, and Andy appeared with a small paper cup in his hand.

"Headache?" he asked. "Here you go."

He handed the cup through the bars. Joe grabbed the deputy's wrist and pulled it so that Andy was brought up hard against the bars.

"*Hey!* What are you doing?" Andy cried.

Frank jumped up and reached through the bars. Grabbing Andy's belt, he found the ring of keys the deputy wore and pulled it loose.

"You guys have really done it now," Andy said, furious. "You'll do hard time for this."

Andy struggled with Joe, but Joe's grip was like iron. Frank found the key to the cell and swung the door open. He grabbed Andy when Joe walked out of the cell, then he shoved the deputy through and locked him in.

"Sorry, Andy," Frank said. "I had to do it."

"I thought you two were all right," Andy replied. "Guess I was wrong about that."

"Lucky for us no one else is here tonight," Frank said as they bolted into the sheriff's office.

The Hardys quickly ran out the courthouse door. In front of the building sat a patrol car, and Frank went through the keys until he found the one for the ignition. He started the powerful engine and looked over at Joe, who hesitated near the passenger door.

"Come on!" yelled Frank. "We've done it now, and there's no time to lose."

Joe jumped in, and Frank drove the car out of town, avoiding the main street, where they might be seen. Once they were beyond the city limits, the road was deserted.

Minutes later they rolled up in front of the Prescotts' house and shut off the engine. The house was dark, and not a sound could be heard.

Frank grabbed a nightstick from a bracket by his seat, the only visible weapon.

"Let's go," he said quietly, "and keep the noise down."

They moved silently to the front door and tried the knob. It turned. Joe pushed the door open, and they cautiously moved inside. A voice came from somewhere to their right.

"Freeze! Or we'll shoot you where you stand!"

The Hardys stood stock-still.

"Lights," said the voice.

The lights came on.

Ted Prescott sat in a wheelchair cradling a small-bore rifle. Callie held a baseball bat, and Kerry, who had turned on the lights, held a large carving knife.

"Frank! Joe!" Callie gaped at the brothers. "I don't understand. Did the sheriff let you go?"

"Have you seen anyone out there? Has anything unusual happened?" Frank asked, ignoring Callie's question for the moment.

"No one and nothing," Ted replied. "Callie told us to be ready for trouble, and we did the best we could. But what gives? I thought you were in jail."

"We were," Joe said. "But when we found

that your phone was dead, we decided we'd be more useful here than in a cell. So here we are."

"The phone isn't working?" Kerry exclaimed, and ran to pick up the receiver. She listened a moment and slowly put it down. "Not a sound," she said softly.

"I had planned to call you," Callie said, "but I must have fallen asleep."

"How did you get out?" Ted asked. "Did the sheriff let you go?"

"Not exactly," answered Frank. "Never mind that for now."

"But I do mind," insisted Ted, wheeling his chair forward, closer to Frank. "You . . . you *escaped*, didn't you? Broke out?"

"Calhoun wouldn't listen to reason, and he left town for the night. Andy Flood couldn't go against orders, so . . ." Frank shrugged. "Don't worry, nobody got hurt. We left Andy Flood in a cell, that's all."

"That's all!" Ted was appalled. "That's enough, don't you think? I can't have you getting into that kind of trouble for my sake. I think you should turn yourselves in right away. We'll manage here."

"Ted," said Frank, "I'm absolutely sure that someone is trying to kill you, and that they'll try again tonight. Tomorrow we'll straighten out our legal problems, but for now, Joe and I are going to see to it that you make it through until morning."

Frank turned the lights off. "No sense in making ourselves easy targets."

"I think I'll take a quick look around outside," said Joe, slipping out the front door.

"Don't go far from the house," Ted said.

"Frank," Callie whispered, "are you and Joe in serious trouble?"

"Not if my hunch is right," he answered.

They waited quietly in the dark. Then, from outside, they heard an animal squeal. The sound was cut off abruptly.

Joe heard the noise and decided to go back and tell Frank.

"I didn't see anybody nearby," he reported, "but I heard an animal—"

From Ted's den there was a low whoosh and a flash of bright light. Joe darted to the doorway and saw that the area by Ted's desk was a mass of flame.

The fire spread quickly, eating through the room's wood paneling and racing across the timbered ceiling.

The others crowded in behind Joe, staring.

Ted lunged forward out of his wheelchair. "My papers! All my records! They're in a secret drawer in that desk. You've got to help me."

Frank grabbed him and dragged him back.

"But all my work!" Ted shouted. "I've *got* to save it."

"Kerry!" Frank shouted. "Take your father to the living room."

Joe grabbed a blanket off a bed and took it into the bathroom, where he soaked it thoroughly under the shower. Wrapping himself in it completely, he entered the study to retrieve the papers. He forced himself to ignore the searing heat and approached the desk.

Part of the ceiling crashed down just in front of him. Joe jumped back as it missed his head by inches. A shower of sparks hissed on the blanket, and Joe staggered away from the raging flames and dense smoke. His chest and throat burned with every inhalation.

"No dice," he gasped as he came out of the den, coughing and throwing off the blanket. "Can't get near it."

The house was mostly wood, and it was dry from the arid desert air. It was quickly becoming engulfed in flame.

"It's out of control!" Frank yelled. "There's nothing we can do, and the house will come down on top of us any minute."

"We'd better get outside," Joe wheezed. "I'll drive to the next house and call the fire department."

Callie, Kerry, and Joe went through the front door and out into the cool desert air. Joe sucked in deep breaths to soothe his lungs.

Frank pushed Ted's wheelchair, moving the engineer out of the terrible heat.

"All that work, all the money I've spent," Ted muttered. "Gone. Wasted."

Frank moved the chair quickly across the flagstone patio in front of the house, then he ran back inside to get the rifle. Ted continued to roll himself away from the smoke, but then a front wheel sank into a crack between two of the stones. The momentum of his rolling tilted the chair forward, and Ted fell face first onto the patio.

The crack of a high-powered rifle sounded, and a bullet ripped through the back of the chair, right where Ted had been a second earlier.

Chapter 12

"GET DOWN. NOW!" Joe yelled.

The two girls crouched behind the jeep while Frank and Joe half dragged, half carried Ted to shelter behind the patrol car. Joe flinched as, with a whine, another shot glanced off the flagstones.

The house stood alone at the end of a short road that branched off the main route to Virginia City. Across the street was barren desert country that rose in a gentle slope. The shots had come from there, somewhere slightly above the house.

Joe raised his head just above the top of the car and ducked back as two more shots cracked.

Frank snapped off a shot in the direction of one of the flashes. "Now they know we're armed," he said. "It'll make them much more cautious."

"There are two shooters," Joe whispered, "both with high-powered rifles, probably scoped. They look to be a hundred yards or so apart."

"I'll bet they're surprised to see *us* out here," Frank said. "They were expecting to find two girls and a disabled man. They probably counted on easy pickings."

"Maybe I can run a bluff on them," said Joe. "Make them think we're going to charge them."

Frank got up quickly and fired once. Then he handed the rifle to his brother. "Take off as if you're going to flank them, and fire a couple of shots as you go."

Joe ran out from behind the car, staying low, and fired two shots in the general direction of the gunmen above. He ducked behind the trunk of a rugged bristlecone pine tree. Then, firing once more, he sprinted across the road and flung himself down behind a bush.

Crouching there for a moment, he wondered if a bluff would work. If he made it appear that he was trying to get behind the gunmen, maybe they would choose not to get into close combat and would simply run for it.

He figured the rifle had a couple of shots left and was poised to make another move when he heard hurried footsteps crunching through the sandy soil above him. The footsteps were headed toward the highway.

A minute later an engine revved up, and a vehicle drove off into the night.

Hearing the engine, Frank swung around to check on the other three, who were still hiding behind the jeep. They seemed to be all right.

"Stay put," he whispered. "I'll be right back."

He raced forward silently and joined Joe.

"It sounded as if one of them was just to the left, about fifty yards up," Joe said.

Frank and Joe ran toward the noise Joe had heard. Joe held the rifle at the ready just in case. As they figured, no one was there. Frank's eye was caught by something on the ground, gleaming in the moonlight. He picked up a brass shell casing and held it out to Joe.

"It's a thirty-caliber cartridge," Joe said. "There's another one."

Frank picked it up and pocketed both of them. "When we nail whoever's doing this, maybe these cartridges can help put them away," Frank said softly.

After listening for a few minutes and hearing no sounds, they walked back to the front yard and joined the others. The house was a complete ruin, and parts had already crumbled to smoldering embers and ash.

"They took off," Joe said, "whoever they were."

"The fire," Kerry began, looking at the house with a stunned expression. "How did it start?"

"It had to be arson," Frank replied. "It might

have been set up in Ted's study while you were picking him up at the hospital. Some kind of delayed-action fuse and a firebomb. A good investigator can find evidence."

"They figured that if the fire didn't kill you all, it would drive you out where they could pick you off one by one," Joe said.

"But who are 'they'?" demanded Callie. "Don Douglas and Sarah Wright?"

"Douglas, maybe," said Joe. "Somehow I can't see Ms. Wright camped up there with a high-powered rifle."

"Women can shoot, too," Frank pointed out.

"What about Toby Flint?" Joe asked. "Maybe he's teamed up with Douglas and Sarah."

"I don't think so," Frank said. "I have a hunch about Toby, but we can talk about him later. Where's Mike Wood?"

Ted had been slumped in his chair, looking beaten, but now he straightened. "Mike Wood has been my assistant for years. I don't understand why you're trying to drag him into this. I don't believe he's involved."

"I hope you're right," Frank assured him. "But there are some unanswered questions about Mike." He told them that Wesley Dunne's investigation drew a blank on locating any Mike Wood in Ukiah.

"There are lots of possible explanations for that," Ted replied, but without much spirit.

He looked at the devastated house and said,

"There's no point in calling the fire department now." Ted's voice was deadened, and he looked like a defeated man. "Anyway, they've got what they wanted," he said. "I'm back at square one, and I can't afford to start over from scratch."

"What got burned up in the fire that's so vital?" asked Joe.

"All my records of core samples we'd dug up, the charts I'd made using sound-wave generators, which showed the likeliest location of gold or silver veins, all the paperwork."

"You mean there weren't any copies?" Frank asked.

"We had a set of copies with us in the shaft yesterday when I fell," Ted replied. "But when Mike went down to fetch what we'd left there, he found that they'd fallen into some standing water and been completely ruined. I had planned on making more copies tomorrow."

"Did Mike know of your second set in the secret drawer?" Frank asked.

"No. Nobody knew. With so much resentment toward me in this town, I decided it would be wise to stash them away."

"So that's why Douglas couldn't find them when he broke in," Frank said.

Ted shivered in the chill of the night.

"Where can we take my father?" Kerry demanded. "He needs to be under a roof someplace, and he's still a target for somebody."

"They've finished me, now," Ted said quietly. "I'm no threat to anyone anymore."

"First of all, you're not finished by a long shot," Frank said. "You've had a setback, and that's all it is. You own part of a mine, you have the technique to get gold ore out of it. All you need is an investor and you'll be back in business."

"And that's why you're still in danger," Frank explained. "If the people going after you want to keep the mines closed, then they want you dead. So we need to put you someplace safe."

"I have a thought on that," said someone behind Joe. Whipping his rifle around, Joe pointed it at a dark silhouette walking toward them from the road. Joe peered into the night and shouted, "Hold it right there, whoever you are!"

"Relax. I'm a friend." The figure raised his hands and came closer, where the light of the flames from the house lit up his features. It was Toby Flint.

"So they burned you out, did they?" Toby said. "You're a serious threat to someone, Mr. Prescott. But I have an idea."

Joe lowered the rifle but held on to it. "Where were you for the last hour, while we were being shot at?" Joe asked Toby.

"Wait a second, Joe," said Frank. He turned to Toby Flint. "You said you have an idea. What is it?"

"Take Prescott to my place," replied Toby. "It's out of the way. No one's likely to find him there. He'll be safe."

"Right," said Joe with a smirk. "We can't just hand him over to you."

"I told you, I'm a friend." Toby was annoyed at Joe's suspicions.

"What are you doing here, anyway?" asked Frank. "Just happened to be in the neighborhood at three in the morning?"

"You think I had something to do with this fire?" Toby growled.

Frank shook his head. "Actually, that's not what I think at all. But I do believe that you've been keeping a pretty close watch on Ted, probably since he first arrived here. Your dropping by at this time of the night makes me think my hunch is right."

"You keep talking about a hunch." Joe faced his brother squarely. "All right, spill it. What is the master detective's big secret?"

By now everyone's curiosity was aroused. Even Ted Prescott had come out of his cloud and was staring at Frank eagerly.

"Okay," Frank said, raising his arms in mock surrender. "Here's my theory. Toby Flint isn't Toby Flint at all."

"Would you mind running that by me again?" Callie said, cupping a hand behind her ear.

"Let me finish," Frank insisted. "Wesley Dunne said that he couldn't find any records on

Toby Flint prior to his arrival in Virginia City. That's because he didn't exist before he came to Virginia City.

"And, Joe, you were right about Toby having a secret that he didn't want to talk about.

"There are no records for Toby Flint because he is really Jonas Middleton, the engineer who disappeared ten years ago."

Chapter 13

JOE AND TED swung around to stare at the prospector.

Toby sighed deeply. "Sooner or later I figured someone might find out who I am. I didn't expect it to be a stranger to these parts, let alone a—well, someone your age."

"All right, Frank," Joe said. "How'd you figure it out?"

"It was a lot of little things," Frank said. "He had a way of appearing whenever anything happened to Ted. That meant that either he was involved in the accidents or he had some other interest in you, Ted. If he wasn't an enemy, then he was a friend, for some reason.

"Also, he knew his way around mines. When he showed up at the Kingmaker and helped us get Ted out of the shaft, he knew what he was doing. He had that harness, which wouldn't be of much use to a prospector who pans for gold above ground.

"He knew the depth of the central shaft in the Kingmaker," Frank continued. "And his little library at home pointed to someone with a professional interest in mining. The books were all pretty advanced, and they'd all been used a good deal.

"And then there was that old claim he showed us, carefully preserved in plastic. I thought it might be more than just a souvenir. Tell me, Toby—or should we call you Jonas now?"

"I've gotten used to Toby. Guess I'll still answer to it, for the time being."

"Whose claim *was* it that you showed us?" asked Frank. "Your great-grandfather's?"

"William Middleton was my great-great-grandfather," Toby answered. "He was an early arrival here, just like Sarah Wright's ancestors. He died broke. But his original claim was handed down to me.

"I arrived ten years ago, full of energy and plans, along with my fiancée, Claire. I was an engineer, and I wanted to test the same method Ted's using now. I planned to make old Grandpa Will's diggings a flourishing mine again. I had my life's savings to make it work." Toby paused and looked at Ted.

"I rented the same house you had, Ted, and got to work. But someone didn't like the idea.

"One day, when I'd been in town a month, I found a threatening note in my mailbox. It was unsigned. It said that if I didn't stop what I was doing and clear out, I'd regret it. But I was stubborn. I hid the note from Claire and went on about my business. There were other notes, and I ignored them, too.

"Then one night, some men jumped me. They were wearing hoods. They dragged me to the side of the road, beat me up, and told me it was the last warning."

"But you still didn't quit?" Joe asked.

Toby snorted. "I thought I could tough it out. Claire screamed when she saw my face. I told her I'd had an accident at the mine. I don't think she believed me, but she didn't say anything.

"Two days later she vanished. A paper was tacked to my front door, saying that when I was all packed up and ready to leave town, I'd be told where to find her.

"That did it. I loaded my stuff into the car and waited. A voice on the phone told me Claire was waiting in an abandoned building in Silver City, a ghost town a few miles from here. I found her there, tied up, gagged, and blindfolded."

"What had happened to her?" Frank asked.

"I don't know what they did," said Toby softly. "She wasn't hurt, but her mind . . . she couldn't get over her kidnapping. Things were never the same between us, and she broke off the engagement and left me. I was alone, and I was flat broke. But I knew what I had to do."

Frank noticed that Ted was listening very intently as Toby continued.

"I got a job, and I worked at it long enough to save a little money. Then I let my beard grow and came back to Virginia City as Toby Flint. My hair had gone totally white, and between that and the beard, nobody knew me, especially since I kept to myself. And I swore that, someday, I would find out who had wrecked my life."

"Then Ted showed up with the same thing in mind that you had planned," Joe said.

"Yes. I decided to keep an eye on him," Toby continued. "It was like we were kin, and I thought maybe I would learn who *my* enemy was by seeing who went after *him.*"

"Sarah Wright and Don Douglas were teenagers ten years ago," said Frank. "So they couldn't have driven you out. Have you discovered who's behind all this?"

"No," Toby replied. "All I've learned is that there were greedy people then, and there are greedy people now."

"What I can't figure," Ted burst out, "is *why?* There's enough wealth in gold and silver below the ground around here to make the whole town rich. Why does anyone want the mining stopped? Could anyone be so greedy that a fortune isn't enough, they have to have *ten* fortunes?"

"Some people lose their heads altogether when they get a whiff of gold," said Toby. "It's like there isn't enough money in the world to satisfy them."

"Yes," Frank said, "but the ones who stopped Jonas Middleton ten years back, they don't appear to have been after the gold themselves. At least nobody has tried to dig it out since then. What was *their* motivation?"

"Good question," said Joe. "It looks as if somebody wanted to stop the mines from producing in quantity, for some reason."

Kerry frowned. "That doesn't make any sense. It would be good for everybody if the mining industry started up again. The whole area would benefit."

"You're assuming that the people who forced Toby out of business back then were acting sensibly," Frank pointed out. "Maybe they weren't. What we know is that nobody tried to put Toby's ideas into effect in the ten years since—until Ted, another newcomer, arrived and got the same treatment."

"Anyway," Toby said, looking at Frank and Joe, "you should get moving pretty quick, I think. Whoever is out to get Ted seems more determined than ever. Why not have the girls take him to my place, and the rest of us can go into town and try to straighten out the mess you're in with the sheriff."

"The part about getting Ted under cover sounds good," replied Joe. "But I don't know about making Calhoun change his mind about us. I don't think he'll believe us until we catch the people who are out for Ted and get a confession."

The Hardys lifted Ted into the backseat of the jeep and placed the folded wheelchair beside him. Kerry and Callie sat in front, and the Hardys and Toby got into the patrol car.

"Stay with Ted until we get word to you," Frank said to Callie and Kerry. The two vehicles pulled away from the smoking ruins of the house and drove toward the junction with the main route from Virginia City.

But as they neared the intersection, another patrol car, its siren wailing and lights flashing, roared up and swung itself across the road, completely blocking their path. The front doors swung open, and Sheriff Calhoun and Deputy Andy Flood got out, both of them looking angry.

"Uh-oh," Toby muttered. "Guess we won't have to go looking for the law after all."

Both law officers drew their guns and walked up to the patrol car Frank drove.

"Making a run for it, were you?" the sheriff said with a nasty smile. "I can understand that."

"Sheriff, if you'll just—" Frank began.

The sheriff ignored Frank and continued, as if he were getting great pleasure out of the confrontation. "Let's see, what are the new charges against you now? Unlawful flight to avoid prosecution and grand theft auto to begin with.

"As for your friends, they'll be facing conspiracy charges. I figure you'll be doing some hard time. Andy, get the handcuffs."

"Listen, Sheriff—" Joe began.

Calhoun cut him off. "I'm through listening to you and your brother."

"Andy—" Frank said.

"That's 'Deputy Flood' to you," snapped the younger officer.

"All right," Joe said. "If you still think we belong in jail, take us in. But first, go and take a look at what's left of Ted's house."

"What's left of it?" Calhoun frowned. "Is this some kind of gag?"

"No gag," Frank assured him. "We were coming to find *you* when you found us."

The sheriff hesitated.

Andy spoke quietly. "It won't hurt to look, Sheriff."

The three cars rode back and stopped by the remains of the house. Joe, Frank, and Toby got out of their car and waited while the sheriff walked slowly through the rubble, poking the embers with a boot. Andy followed him. Then the sheriff and deputy came back to the others.

"Okay, tell me," Calhoun said. "What happened here?"

Frank and Joe related the events of that night, including Ted's close call with the bullet. Andy's glare softened as he listened, and even Calhoun's face grew thoughtful.

"I'll have some state people come up from Carson City," said Calhoun. "They'll find out if it was arson soon enough."

Frank fished the two brass cartridge cases out of his pocket. "These are from the guns that fired at us," he said. "Maybe you'll be able to match them up once you find who's responsible."

Calhoun took the cartridges.

"Something else you should know," said Toby Flint, coming forward. "You recall the story of that engineer, Jonas Middleton, who went missing ten years ago?"

The sheriff nodded.

"Well, he's not missing anymore."

Calhoun gaped. "What do you mean?"

"I'm Jonas Middleton," Toby replied. "I was driven out of town by a combination of scare tactics and assault. I couldn't get the law to pay any attention to *my* problems, either."

"Sheriff," said Andy Flood, "mistakes were made here, and we have to see that they're corrected. You see that, don't you? You've been wrong about these people."

"I suppose," Calhoun said quietly. He looked at the others. "I'm not used to doing this," he said, "but I think I have to apologize to you all. I let certain people influence me, people with power."

"You mean Sarah?" Frank asked.

The sheriff nodded. "Sarah asked me to keep you and your brother out of the way. That's why

I didn't help you with your investigation in the beginning. She convinced me you were meddlers. And she persuaded me to let Don go, since we didn't find his fingerprints on anything at Prescott's place.

"I was once a good law officer," Calhoun continued. "It's time I became one again. Running Sarah and Don in will be a step in that direction."

"Can I make a suggestion?" asked Frank.

"Go ahead," Calhoun answered.

"I don't think Sarah and Don alone are responsible for everything that's happened in the last few days. There has to be at least one other culprit at large."

"So?" prompted the sheriff.

"So right now they still think you believe their story," Frank went on. "Let's use them."

"Right!" Joe said. "We can set a trap to bring their partners out into the open."

"I don't know," said Calhoun. "It goes against the grain not to arrest suspected felons right away."

"If you take them and let the others go free," Frank pointed out, "Ted and Kerry will still be in danger. Better to grab them all at once."

"You have something in mind?" asked Calhoun.

Frank explained his idea. Joe added some details. And Calhoun, after making a few objections and changes of his own, agreed.

Chapter 14

FRANK, JOE, the sheriff, and Andy drove to the courthouse to set the plan in motion. The town was just beginning to stir as they arrived. Ted, Toby, Kerry, and Callie went off to get some breakfast at a café on C Street and planned to go to Toby's from there.

At the sheriff's office, the first thing Calhoun did was pick up a phone and dial Sarah Wright's number. The Hardys listened as he spoke.

"Morning, Sarah, this is Sheriff Calhoun. I'd appreciate it if you and Don could drop by my office soon. I've drawn up formal charges against the Hardys, and once you sign the papers, I can start moving on an indictment. . . . Half an hour? That'll be perfect. See you both then. Thank *you*, Sarah."

The sheriff hung up. "All set." He turned to Andy. "Deputy, work up some official-looking documents for those two to sign when they arrive. We'll make it look like we're doing this by the book."

The sheriff served the Hardys some coffee and doughnuts while they waited, and the three of them discussed the plan further.

When Sarah Wright and Don Douglas entered the office, Frank and Joe sat on a wooden bench, handcuffed to the arms. Douglas smirked at them as he sat down in front of Calhoun's desk. The sheriff gave Sarah and Don the forms Andy had supplied.

"Hear about the trouble at Ted Prescott's house last night?" the sheriff asked casually.

Don didn't look up from the form he was reading, but Sarah did, quickly.

"Trouble? What happened?" she asked.

"His house was burned down, and then someone shot at Ted. Luckily he's okay. But the fire was arson, meant to drive him out to where he could be an easy target."

Frank and Joe watched as Sarah turned pale and stole a look at Douglas, by her side.

"Don!" she exclaimed.

He gave her a flat, expressionless stare.

"Did you . . . did you hear what the sheriff said. Isn't that awful?"

Douglas kept his eyes fixed on Sarah. "Terrible," he replied. Then he signed the complaint form. "Sign your name, honey."

"I imagine," the sheriff went on, "that it was done to force Mr. Prescott to stop his work. It's lucky he has another copy of his records, so he can get back to work once his health permits."

Now Don looked up sharply. "That's good to hear," he said.

Andy took the papers that Don and Sarah had signed. He spoke casually. "Yeah, he says he hid the papers in a little metal box in the Kingmaker tunnel just yesterday. His daughter helped him."

"Andy, don't talk about Mr. Prescott's business," the sheriff scolded. He smiled at Sarah and Don. "We can trust you two to keep this confidential, right?"

"Absolutely," said Douglas, standing abruptly. "Is that all, Sheriff? We're in kind of a hurry."

"That'll do it," said Calhoun.

Don almost ran out of the office. As soon as Sarah closed the door behind her, Andy unlocked the brothers' handcuffs.

Rubbing his wrists, Joe said, "Don rushed out of here like a man with a purpose."

"He was in a hurry, all right," Andy agreed.

"I still don't know if I care for the idea of you two staking out that mine," said Calhoun.

"It's like we told you, we're good at that kind of thing," Joe replied. "And we'll have that radio with us so we can get in touch as soon as something happens."

"Well, that's true," Calhoun said, opening a closet and dragging out a military-style wireless radio. "These are supposed to have a range of several miles. We'll stay in touch."

"Think of us as deputies," Frank said. "We'll just stop over to see Callie, Ted, and the others, and tell the girls to hide out at Toby's shack for safekeeping. Then we'll head out there and find some good cover."

They were testing the radio when Andy, looking out the window, said, "Sarah's coming this way. Should I put those cuffs back on?"

"No, you two can listen from over here," said Calhoun, opening the door between the office and the jail cells. The Hardys went through, and Calhoun left the door open just enough for them to see and hear.

Sarah Wright came in and sat across from the sheriff. Peering through the crack in the door, Frank saw that she had been crying. She twisted a handkerchief between her fingers and took a deep shuddering breath.

"I don't know how to say what I have to say," she began. "I . . . I've been a fool."

"Take your time, Sarah," Calhoun said. "Can I get you anything—a glass of water?"

"No, thank you." She pushed back her dark hair and went on. "I have a confession to make. Those two young men—they didn't do anything in my house. When they said that we had an appointment with them, they were telling the truth."

"Why did you lie, Sarah?" asked the sheriff.

"It was Don's idea. He's been telling me that I had to stand up for what was rightfully mine, and that I was crazy to let an outsider with a trumped-up claim come here and take my land. He said that if we could get the Hardys out of the way for a while, he would be able to put some real pressure on Ted Prescott and make him give up his plans. I had no idea that Don would go so far as to try killing someone." Sarah paused and sighed deeply.

"When we left here, I demanded that he tell me whether he had been a part of last night's goings-on. When he wouldn't answer, I accused him of being involved. He said I was a fool, and that I was too weak to take what I wanted. He said that he was only marrying me for my money. . . ." Sarah bit her lip. "Then he told me to get out of the car, right in the middle of the street, that he had no more time to waste on me, and he drove away." She started to cry again.

The sheriff handed her a tissue, and she thanked him in a choked voice.

"Actually, Sarah," said Calhoun, "we already knew that you'd framed Frank and Joe." He motioned the Hardys into the room. "We were doing a little playacting so we could find out, among other things, how deeply *you* might be involved in the attempts to kill Ted Prescott."

She stared at Calhoun and the Hardys in turn. "You've *got* to believe me. I'm no murderer. I was a fool, I can see that, but I'm not crazy enough to try to kill someone."

"What about Don?" Joe asked. "Do you know if he sabotaged Ted's equipment in the mine shaft or tampered with his oxygen tank at the hospital? And was he really with you yesterday at the parade when someone shot at Frank?"

"Yes, he was with me," said Sarah. "But I don't know if he's responsible for trying to murder Ted. I really don't know him at all, I'm afraid."

"So we know that there's at least one more would-be murderer to be found," said Frank.

"What will happen to me?" asked Sarah.

"The fact that you came forward as you did will help," the sheriff said. "But you have to keep what you've just heard completely confidential. And if all you did was make a false accusation against the Hardys, I won't be too hard on you."

With an apologetic smile at Frank and Joe, she thanked the sheriff and left the office.

"We'd better get moving," said Joe. "Don Douglas is going to tell someone about the extra set of papers, and he won't waste any time."

Andy Flood drove them to the café to tell Callie and the others of the plan, then out to the

Kingmaker mine, so that no telltale vehicle would have to be left in the area. They took the wireless radio along with a knapsack of food and tools and two canteens full of water. It was getting into the hot part of the day when they arrived at the mine. Joe looked out and frowned at the heat waves shimmering over the landscape.

"Good hunting," said Andy with a wave as he drove away.

Frank and Joe waved back, then surveyed the terrain by the tunnel entrance more closely. Sand-colored hills rose around them, and vegetation was sparse.

"We need some fairly flat ground with at least some bushes for cover," Frank said, shading his eyes with his hand.

"Wait a minute, I think I've spotted a place." Joe pointed up the steep rise directly over the tunnel mouth. "There, about twenty feet above the entrance and ten yards to the right."

Frank looked up. "It looks good," he said. "Let's go see."

Joe led the way up the sheer slope to a level place about eight feet square. He noted that it was fairly well screened from anyone below by a thicket.

"This is it," Joe announced. "Let's make ourselves at home."

He pulled a small shovel from the pack and scraped a depression in the sandy soil. He smoothed out the surface so that they could lie motionless and not be too uncomfortable. Meanwhile, Frank stowed the knapsack and canteens under the bushes so that they were in partial shade.

"There's enough shade here for one of us, so we can switch off," he said.

"All the comforts," Joe replied, putting the shovel back in the pack. "You take the shade first. I'll just take a little nap here in the sunshine. Work on my tan."

"That's what vacations are for," Frank said. "Don't let me get in your way." He stretched out in the shade.

Joe pulled a pair of sunglasses from the pack and found a spot from which he had a view of the clearing below through the vegetation. He and Frank settled down to wait.

"I sure hope somebody shows up soon," Joe muttered half an hour later, wiping sweat off his forehead. "Not that I mind the sweltering heat or anything."

After another half hour Frank moved into the sun, and Joe crawled into the shade with a sigh. Joe took a drink from a canteen. In the shade the heat wasn't so unbearable. He was almost asleep when Frank's voice snapped him awake.

"We have company. Get Calhoun on the radio."

Joe grabbed the unit from next to the pack and switched it on. He spoke softly into the mouthpiece.

"Hello, Central, this is Desert Fox. Desert Fox calling Central, come in."

There was no answer from the receiver. Joe tried again, but heard only a faint hissing sound.

"Something's wrong with this radio," he whispered to his brother. "I'm not getting anything, and I can't be sure we're sending, either. How much company is there?"

"Just two," Frank replied. "Check it out."

Joe crept to where he could see through the undergrowth. Two men were getting out of a big all-terrain vehicle. As they approached the tunnel entrance, Joe could see they had powerful flashlights and were both armed with pistols stuck into their belts. One was Don Douglas.

And Joe was stunned to see the other was Mike Wood.

Chapter 15

"CAN YOU BELIEVE IT?" Joe whispered to his brother. "Mike Wood is in on this."

Frank shook his head and looked down at the two men. "Ted's going to have a hard time believing it, I'll tell you that. But Wood's had the opportunity to go after Ted, if any one has."

"That's for sure," Joe said.

"You can't raise anybody on that radio?" Frank asked. "It was working in Calhoun's office."

"Maybe its range isn't enough after all," Joe whispered back. "Or maybe we're getting through to them but they can't talk to us because there's a glitch in the receiver. There's no way to know, and no time to mess around with it."

Below them, Wood and Douglas were getting

out picks and excavating gear. The Hardys continued to talk in whispers.

"Why all the gear?" Joe asked. "What are they going to do, dig for gold once they're down there?"

"Maybe they figure the papers are well hidden. The sheriff didn't tell them exactly where to look."

"I think we can take both guys," Joe said. "We have surprise on our side."

"They have guns on their side," Frank answered, leaning farther forward to keep Don and Mike in view.

"We can jump them," urged Joe. "Between the flashlights and the digging gear, their hands are full. We'll be on them before they can go for their guns."

"I just can't see either of these two as the brains behind the whole plot," Frank said.

"Well, these are the two we've got." Joe was eager to move. "Let's take them down, and if Calhoun doesn't show up in a few minutes with his men, we'll bring Wood and Douglas in ourselves. If they have a boss, maybe we can persuade one of them to turn him in."

Frank nodded. "Okay, let's go. I'll take Douglas, you go for Mike."

They crouched, still unobserved by the men below, and began to scramble down at the same time. Then Joe launched himself forward and was momentarily airborne as he dropped downward. He slammed into Mike Wood from the side and knocked him to the ground.

Frank took a step forward, then began to slide, and his right foot twisted beneath him. There was a flash of pain in his ankle, and he fell, rolling down the hill and landing almost at Don Douglas's feet. The impact of the fall knocked the wind out of him and left him dazed.

Douglas, astonished at first, quickly dropped his pick and clawed an automatic from his belt. As Frank struggled to his knees, Don stepped in and drove a heavy boot into his side. Frank collapsed on the ground.

Joe was on top of Mike, trying to grab the man's gun, when he saw Don put the barrel of the huge .45 automatic against Frank's ear.

"Hold it right there, or I'll put a big hole in your brother's skull!" Don bellowed.

Joe raised both hands and stood slowly.

Mike Wood rose, coughing, and pulled out his gun. He pointed it at Joe. "You almost broke my shoulder," Mike said.

"Oh, I'm sorry," Joe retorted. "Next time I'll go for the other shoulder."

Mike swung a looping left that caught Joe on the cheekbone. Joe's head snapped around, and he felt a hot pain, but he remained standing.

Mike swung around and glared at Douglas. "You told me these two were in jail. They were out of the picture, you said."

"Well, I thought they were!" Don went over

to Frank, reached down, and hauled him upright. He grabbed the front of Frank's shirt and held the gun under his chin.

"What gives?" Don demanded. "How come you're not in the lockup? Come on, spit it out."

"We got time off for good behavior," Frank said. He put some weight on his right foot, to test it. There was pain, but he knew no bones were broken. He thought it might be a sprain.

Don's face went bright red, and he jammed the barrel of the gun hard into Frank's stomach. Frank gasped, and his legs felt wobbly for a moment.

"I owe you already, wise guy!" Don yelled. "You cut out the smart mouth, or I'm going to pound on you till you wish for a nice quick bullet."

"The sheriff found out we weren't guilty," Joe shouted.

Don frowned. Then he nodded. "Sure! *Sarah* went and told him everything she knew, to save herself from going to jail. I'll deal with her later."

Joe decided to try buying time. He looked at Mike with puzzlement. "I don't understand you, Mike. From what I heard, Ted Prescott trained you for a career and gave you steady work. How can you turn around and do this to him and Kerry?"

Mike flushed, opened his mouth to speak, and then looked away without saying anything.

Don Douglas let out a loud, harsh laugh. "You mean you don't know about the skeleton in Mike's closet? Wood's got a deep, dark secret, and he'll do anything to keep it that way."

"Shut up!" Mike yelled, but Don paid no attention. His contempt for Mike showed in his face as he continued.

"Our Mike here is a desperate criminal. He's on the run from the United States Army. That's right, he's a deserter. If they ever catch up with him—"

"I'm warning you, Don!" Mike screamed, ignoring Joe and fixing Douglas with a furious stare. "You keep your mouth shut about me, or—"

"Or *what*, tough guy?" sneered Don. "What are you gonna do about it? You don't have the guts to shoot me, and you wouldn't dare try to fight me."

He glared at Mike, challenging him, and Mike turned away first.

Don laughed again. "It's a tough life in military prison, from what I hear," he said. "You couldn't stand up to it, boy. You don't have what it takes. And it could be years before you got out."

Mike suddenly whirled around, his gun pointed at Don. "*All right!* I warned you!"

Frank and Joe saw the opportunity at the same time. Joe grabbed Mike's extended arm and brought it up sharply behind his back. Mike screamed in pain and dropped the gun on the ground. Joe picked it up and trained it on Wood.

Frank pivoted on his right foot and sent a karate kick into Don's midsection, and Don doubled over with a grunt. Ignoring the sudden pain in his injured foot, Frank chopped at the base of his opponent's neck, and Don crumbled to the ground.

Then Frank scooped up the dropped pistol. "You okay?" he called to Joe.

"Yeah," Joe answered. "Never been better. How's your ankle?"

"Sprained, I think." Frank flexed it carefully and winced.

"I'll try the radio again," said Joe. "You watch these two for a second." He climbed back up to where they had left the equipment, but got no better results with the radio than before.

"No luck," he said, after clambering back down. "It looks as if we'll have to take these two into town without any backup."

"Listen," Douglas said. "I have a proposition for you two."

"Not interested," Frank said. He gestured with the automatic for Douglas to walk toward the all-terrain vehicle.

Douglas didn't go. "Now, wait a minute." Douglas grinned at Frank, trying to look friendly. "There's a fortune down in that mine just waiting for somebody with the guts to go get it. Why couldn't it be us? Frank. Joe. You're both tough. We'd make a great combination. We'd all be rich! What do you say, huh?"

"What about Ted Prescott?" Joe asked, with a deadpan look at Frank.

"We can get rid of Prescott, no problem," said Don. "He's nothing to you, right?"

"And what about Sarah Wright? And Sheriff Calhoun?" asked Frank.

"Hey, I'll sweet-talk Sarah. She's still crazy about me. As for the sheriff, we can let him in on the deal. Money talks, right?"

"Not to us," said Joe. "No deal, Douglas."

Don cursed and kicked angrily at a stone.

"All the attempts to kill Ted," Joe said, looking at Mike. "His fall in the mine shaft, the oxygen tank business, the arson and shooting last night—you were responsible for that, right?"

Mike nodded. Then he looked up and pointed to Douglas. "But last night *he* was there, too. *He* was a part of it. It wasn't just me!" He stared angrily at Don Douglas.

"That's right, Wood, spill your guts out," Don said, his voice dripping with scorn.

"I *told* you to shut up about my past!" Mike yelled. "You wouldn't listen. Now I'm going to see to it that you do as much jail time as I do!"

It was obvious to Frank that Douglas and Wood weren't working as partners against Ted. And Frank doubted that either one was the mastermind behind the scheme. He decided to try calling them on his hunch.

"It'll go easier on you both if you name the one responsible for all this," Frank said. "Mike, tell the sheriff who made you do what you did and you might get a break."

The blast of a shotgun rang out behind them.

"No one will be telling the sheriff anything about anybody," a voice said. "Turn around slowly and don't do anything foolish."

As Frank, Joe, and the others turned, they saw that a car had been parked in back of the all-terrain vehicle. Standing in front of it were Ted and Kerry Prescott and Callie Shaw, all looking frightened and pale.

Behind them, with his shotgun aimed point-blank at Kerry's head, was Brandon Jessup.

Chapter 16

FRANK AND JOE, both amazed that Jessup was behind the murderous plans, exchanged a stunned glance.

"Mr. Jessup!" called Mike Wood. "It's not my fault! Don started riding me about the army, and I got mad and—"

"Be quiet," Jessup snarled. His voice wasn't loud, but Mike shut his mouth.

"I'll hear from you later, Mike," Jessup went on. "First things first. Frank, Joe, toss those guns toward me. I don't have to tell you what will happen to Miss Prescott if you don't obey me."

The Hardys did as they were told, throwing the automatics a few feet from Jessup.

"Sorry, Frank," Callie said. "We ran into Mr.

Jessup in town, and he looked so sympathetic about Kerry's father that when he offered us a ride out to Toby's place, we agreed. And then he brought us here."

"It's okay, Callie," Frank replied. "Just take it as easy as you can."

Don Douglas started forward to pick up the weapons.

"Stay where you are, Don," Jessup said. "Mike, you get the guns. Come on now, quickly."

Don froze. Looking fearfully at Jessup, he said, "Hey, what gives here? I'm on your side. I did what you told me, didn't I?"

"I don't trust you, Don," Jessup replied, as Mike scrambled to grab the guns. "You're greedy, and you're a bully. You and Mike were sent here as a team, but you wouldn't follow orders. You had to give Mike a hard time and get him upset. You almost ruined everything.

"I trust Mike. He will always do what I say because he knows what will become of him if he doesn't."

"Aw, come on, Mr. Jessup," Don wheedled. "I was just having some fun."

"Your 'fun' allowed those two young men to get the drop on you. If I hadn't shown up here when I did, who knows what would have happened? From here on in, you will do *exactly* what you're told, or you'll suffer the consequences. Do I make myself clear?"

"Yes, sir, Mr. Jessup," Don muttered.

Jessup gestured with the shotgun for Frank and Joe to move closer to the tunnel mouth. He directed the Prescotts and Callie to join them, and then gave Don Douglas a long, hard stare.

"All right, Mike," he said at length. "Give Don a pistol. But I'm watching you, Don. If you do anything suspicious, you're dead." Then he turned back to his prisoners.

"*Why,* Jessup?" Joe demanded. "What's the point of this? You want the mine all for yourself?"

"You think it's gold I'm after. I understand that. People are greedy." Jessup frowned. "But I am different. For generations my people have served as shopkeepers for all the lucky souls who struck gold in these beautiful mountains. We shipped in food from the East, we served them, we brought in bolts of cotton. . . . Everything the miner used in Virginia City, my family provided through hard work. And what do we have to show for it?"

He looked around, his eyes blazing. "A few measly shops in a little tourist town, while the people we slaved for languish in their mansions, counting their acres of land and the deeds to their mines.

"What would happen if the mines began operating again?" Jessup continued. "It would mean wealth, true. But wealth only for the very same landowners, the very same miners who did nothing their whole lives but get lucky, while the little man did all the work for them."

"Jessup," Frank said, "you already own half the businesses in this town. What more do you want?"

Jessup chuckled. "Yes, the tourist trade brings me a comfortable living," he said. "But I deserve more! Virginia City owes me a lot. What these mine owners don't know is that I've been quietly buying parcels of land just outside town over the past ten years. Only *I* know the details of the spectacular wild West theme park that is planned for this town. It's been hard not to tell everyone for miles around what I'm planning. But I've kept my mouth shut. Because this time I'm not going to share the wealth. It's going to be mine," he added grimly. "But Prescott's land here borders on the land I've been accumulating for the theme park. There's no room in my plan for a working mine, with its noisy machinery and dust and pollution."

"He's crazy," Callie murmured.

Jessup scowled. "You think I'm crazy, do you? There's nothing wrong with me! I just want what's owed to my family. When Prescott arrived with his instruments and charts, I knew he would have to be stopped.

"I used my contacts as a journalist to find out all I could about him and his assistant. I even got their fingerprints by buying them drinks in my café and sending the glasses to an expert. Imagine my delight when I found that Mike had a shameful secret in his past and was wanted under another name. I knew I had the tool to take care of Prescott. Does that sound like the logic of a crazy man?

"Mike told me that Prescott's mining method was successful. So I had to move fast. At my orders, Mike sabotaged that scaffold in the shaft. He went back and hid the cut rope that he had been stupid enough to leave behind. He tampered with the oxygen tank at the hospital.

"And each attempt failed! Because you meddlers chose to get mixed up where you had no business. So I ordered Mike to scare you away. But the rattlesnake didn't do it, nor did the boulders that almost crushed your car."

"Let me guess," said Joe. "Mike was the masked bank robber who shot at Frank."

"Right-on, my boy," Jessup replied. "If he was hit, well and good. If not, it was meant to discourage you two. But you were stubborn as well as meddlesome.

"So I brought in Don Douglas. He had been trying, in his own foolish way, to drive Prescott out. I should have known he was worthless when he got caught looking for Prescott's papers. But Douglas saw the genius of my plan and agreed to help me kill Prescott. And you two young men ignored my hints to get out, so you will share his fate. The central shaft of the Kingmaker mine will be your tomb."

Callie and Frank exchanged a worried glance.

"In a few years, I *will* reopen the mines,"

Jessup went on. "But on a small scale, just enough to satisfy my clients' needs. But I need Prescott's records. I was afraid they were lost forever, until Don told me today of the extra copy hidden in the tunnel."

Jessup walked toward the group of captives. Joe listened to his ramblings with a growing worry that they were dealing with a mixture of madness and greed that could easily blow up in their faces.

"You," said Jessup, pointing with the barrel of the shotgun at Ted Prescott, who was being supported by his daughter. "I must have those papers You will tell me where they are."

"I can't do that, Jessup," the engineer replied, his eyes on the gun.

"And I say you have to!" Jessup shouted.

"Why should he help you?" Frank asked. "You've told us we're going to be killed, in any event."

"Cover them, you two," Jessup snapped to his henchmen.

He reached forward and pulled Kerry Prescott toward him. Ted, deprived of her support, staggered. Frank quickly grabbed the engineer's arm and steadied him.

"You will tell me where those papers are hidden," Jessup shouted, "or you will watch your daughter die before your eyes. Choose."

"Wait!" shouted Ted. "Listen to me! Jessup,

there *are* no other copies. The only ones I had were destroyed in the fire last night."

"I know otherwise," Jessup said. "Don't try to fool me. The sheriff told Don about the extra copies you hid in the tunnel. I'm losing patience. Where are they?"

"Ted is telling you the truth," Frank said. "We made up the story of the extra copies to bring you out into the open, that's all. Ted has no copies. The papers were burned in the fire—the one your men set."

"You expect me to believe that?" shouted Jessup, wrapping one arm around Kerry's neck. "Do you think I'm a fool? Tell me where you hid them. You have ten seconds."

Frank sensed that something had to be done right away to distract the crazed man. He looked at Mike Wood and Don Douglas, who both appeared nervous.

"Mike! Don!" Frank shouted desperately. "This guy is totally insane. He might shoot you, too, if he thinks you're a threat. No one's been killed yet. There's still time to stop him."

Keeping his grip on Kerry, Jessup stepped toward Frank and swung the barrel of the shotgun at him in a backhanded slash. Frank saw it coming and started to spin away, but it caught him where his neck and shoulder met.

He felt a hot flash of pain and fell heavily to the ground next to the tools that Don and Mike had dropped. His dodge had been just enough to avoid the full impact of the blow, and he remained conscious, but his arms and legs felt like rubber and he couldn't move.

Seeing Frank go down, Joe took a single step forward but stopped as Jessup swung his shotgun and aimed it at Joe's chest.

"Prescott!" Jessup yelled. "For the last time—where are those papers?"

"I'm telling you the truth, man," Ted pleaded. "*There are no papers*. If there were, don't you think I'd hand them over?"

"Very well, Prescott," Jessup snapped, and flung Kerry down on the ground. He raised the shotgun and jacked a shell into the chamber.

He put the barrel against her head.

Chapter 17

"BRANDON JESSUP!" a voice boomed from out of the still desert air.

Toby Flint emerged from behind the cars and walked toward the mine entrance. Everyone froze in place, staring at him in surprise. He passed by Mike and Don without a glance, keeping his gaze focused on Jessup.

Momentarily confused, Jessup looked up at Toby. "Flint! What are you doing here? Are you out of your mind?"

"If I am," said Toby, advancing slowly toward the man with the shotgun, "that would make two of us, wouldn't it, Mr. Jessup?"

Jessup forgot about the girl huddled at his feet and aimed the shotgun at the prospector. "Keep your distance, Flint. Stop right where you are."

Flint slowly shook his head and came forward a few more steps. Joe looked from one man to the other. It seemed that Toby's unblinking stare, fixed on Jessup, had almost hypnotized him.

"Jessup," Flint said at last, coming to a stop ten feet from the man, "I have a surprise for you."

"What . . . what are you talking about? Why did you come here?" Jessup asked, scowling.

Joe flicked a quick glance at Don and Mike. They stood as if nailed to the ground. It was clear to Joe that neither of the two had any idea of how to handle Jessup.

Frank got to his hands and knees and shook his head to clear it. As his vision returned, his eye fell on a pick that Don had dropped. It had a wooden handle two feet long and a double-headed blade of sharpened steel. The handle was only a few feet from him.

"I've come from out of your past, Brandon Jessup," said Toby.

It's as if there's no one here but Toby and Jessup, thought Joe. The gaping barrel of the shotgun seemed to mean nothing to Toby. And Jessup was definitely spooked by the unexpected appearance of the man, and by his unwavering stare.

"Out of my *past?*" echoed Jessup.

"I've been waiting for this for a long, long

time. Ten years, to be exact. Do you remember? Do you place me now?"

Jessup opened his mouth, but no words came out. He shook his head and stared.

"I'll give you a little hint, Mr. Jessup. I'm not as old as I look. Ten years ago, I was a young man. I had hopes and dreams. I had a young lady whom I loved and planned to marry. But you put an end to it all."

From his knees, Frank looked up at his brother, who met his eyes. Frank risked a quick look at the pick lying on the ground, and Joe saw it, then gave his brother a slight nod. Frank remained on his hands and knees, acting more dazed and helpless than he was. Neither Toby nor Jessup paid any attention to him.

Jessup took a deep breath. "I don't know what you mean, Flint."

"Don't call me Flint, Mr. Jessup. The time has come for you to call me by the name I was born with. That's the least you can do for me, after all. You had me threatened and then beaten up. You kidnapped my fiancée, and she never recovered from that. Neither did I, really. . . ."

Recognition suddenly dawned in Jessup's face. "Middleton!" he whispered, his eyes wide.

"That's right, Mr. Jessup. A beard and white hair changes a man, doesn't it? My hair went completely white just after I left Virginia City, so I guess I have you to thank for it. I came back, Mr. Jessup. I came back to find out who's to blame for destroying my whole life. And now I've found him."

Though Jessup was armed and Toby Flint wasn't, the older man took a step back. He looks like a man who has just seen a ghost, Frank decided, and that must be the way he feels.

Frank slowly moved his right hand a little closer to the pick handle. In stepping back from Flint, Jessup had gotten a bit closer to his prisoners.

"It's all over, Mr. Jessup," said Toby, moving a step closer. "You're done for."

"What do you mean by that, Flint?"

"To you, my name is Jonas Middleton!" The prospector's voice lashed out, and Jessup cringed at the sound of it.

"I mean that I'll see to it that everyone knows you for what you are," Toby continued. "You'll end your days in a jail cell, despised by all the people who once respected you."

Toby took another step forward. As he did, Frank's hand crept six inches closer to the pick.

Brandon Jessup's face was set in a crazed mask of hate, lips drawn back and teeth clenched. His hands, which had begun to shake, now steadied on the shotgun.

"I should have had you killed ten years ago, Middleton," he snarled. "Now I can correct that error in judgment."

Frank launched himself forward and grabbed

the pick handle. Pivoting and rising to his feet, he swung the pick underhanded. The blade flashed up and smashed into Jessup's left arm, sending the gun barrel up in the air just as Jessup's finger squeezed the trigger.

The bullets passed harmlessly over Toby's head, and the deafening blast of the weapon almost drowned out Jessup's cry of pain as he dropped the gun and gripped his injured arm.

"Don! Mike!" he shrieked. "Shoot them! Now!"

Joe dived for Jessup's shotgun, grabbed it, and jumped to his feet, jacking a shell into the chamber as he did. But Don Douglas was quick to realize that things weren't going his way. Rather than stand and shoot it out against a shotgun, he ran for Jessup's car, which was faster than his own vehicle. He leapt in, turned the ignition key, and backed out of the clearing in a cloud of dust. He swung the car around, banging into a rock in the process, and took off for the highway, leaving a trail of burned rubber behind him.

"I'm not gonna go to jail!" yelled Mike Wood, pointing his gun at Joe and letting off two wild shots. Joe dived and rolled to his left, then fired from a prone position. Mike screamed as a bullet struck his hand and the pistol flew out of it.

"Let's get Douglas," Frank called, sprinting for the jeep.

Joe handed the shotgun to Toby Flint. "Think you can watch these creeps for a few minutes?"

Toby smiled and took the gun. "It'll be my pleasure. Go get him!"

Joe detoured to pick up Mike's automatic and jumped into the passenger seat of the jeep. Frank whirled it in a tight U-turn and roared off in pursuit of Douglas.

"He'll be on the road to Virginia City!" Joe yelled, pitching his voice to be heard over the noise of the wind howling through the open jeep.

"No sweat!" Frank shouted back. "He's only got a thirty-second lead. That big boat of Jessup's isn't built for maneuvering."

He swung out into the road to avoid a clump of thorny bushes and barely slowed as he squealed onto the highway. Seconds later they spotted Jessup's luxury sedan as it topped a rise half a mile ahead. Douglas was having trouble controlling the car as he took the curves of the road, the rear end fishtailing badly. The jeep's better balance and Frank's skill as a driver allowed the Hardys to eat up the gap between themselves and Douglas.

There was no other traffic on the road, and Frank was able to follow the twists and turns with little braking. Before long, Douglas's lead had been cut in half, and soon Joe could make out Don's panicky face as he sneaked looks over his shoulder at his pursuers.

Frank kept his eyes glued to the road. Just

before it reached flat desert terrain and straightened out, it turned in a particularly sharp hairpin curve. Only yards ahead, Don took the curve too fast, and the sedan skidded off the pavement. The car hit a patch of deep sand. In seconds its rear wheels were buried up to the hubcaps.

As Don floored the gas pedal, desperately trying to free himself, Frank pulled the jeep up alongside him and slammed on the brakes. "Get out of the car," he ordered.

But Douglas climbed out on the passenger's side and crouched behind the car, pistol in hand.

Frank and Joe dived from their seats as Douglas fired a shot that shattered the windshield where Frank had been sitting. Another bullet whined, caroming off the body of the car.

"Give it up, Douglas!" called Joe. "Your friends are through, and you are, too. All you're doing is adding years to the sentence you'll be getting."

In reply, Don shot again, and a bullet whined over Frank's head.

"We can wait you out, Douglas," Frank shouted. "A state trooper or a sheriff's car will be along sooner or later."

Suddenly Don jumped up and dashed across the road toward the hills. Staying in a crouch, Joe darted from behind the jeep to the shelter of Jessup's car. Don spun around and let two more shots fly, and then took off running again.

"Let me take him!" Joe shouted back to Frank.

Frank, who now carried Mike Wood's gun, waved a signal of understanding and held his own fire. Joe raced across the road, zigzagging to avoid any gunfire, and ducked behind a clump of bushes.

Joe counted four more reports from Don's weapon, but the shots went wild. As Joe broke cover, Don raised his pistol again, but no shot was heard. He threw the empty pistol aside and ran once more.

Don, for all his muscles, did not have the stamina Joe had. Douglas slogged up the sandy hill, gasping for breath. He began to stagger while Joe kept to a steady ground-eating pace that he knew he could maintain for miles.

Then Joe was on Douglas's heels. With a diving tackle, Joe slammed Douglas to the ground. Don kicked back, and a boot heel struck Joe a jolting blow on the shoulder. Douglas crawled out of Joe's grip and got to his feet, but he had no real fight left in him.

He threw a single desperate roundhouse right as Joe came forward, but Joe easily ducked inside it. His own right uppercut traveled less than a foot before connecting solidly with Douglas's jaw. Don went down and stayed there.

Joe yanked Douglas to his feet and twisted his right arm behind his back. Wordlessly he marched him back to where Frank waited with the jeep.

Frank studied the panting Douglas, whose face was bright red from his effort.

"While you're in jail," Frank said, "try to spend less time lifting weights and do some running instead."

Ten minutes later the Hardys pulled up to the mine, with their prisoner in the back of the jeep. Sheriff Calhoun had already arrived with two patrol cars full of deputies, including Andy Flood.

As Andy took charge of the sullen criminals, Calhoun came over to the others. "Everybody here all right?" he asked.

"We're all okay," Frank answered. "Which is more than I can say for your radios."

The sheriff looked sheepish. "The salesman at the surplus store said they'd do the job," he said. "I can't understand it."

"Try spending a little more money next time," Joe suggested.

"I'll take statements in town," Calhoun said. "Follow me back to the office."

Some time later, as the last of the statements was being transcribed for signatures, Jessup was locked in a cell, along with Mike and Don. The sheriff walked back into his office just as Sarah Wright arrived.

"I have some apologies to make," she said. "I've realized that my family pride turned me into a fool."

"No apologies are necessary," Frank replied.

Sarah looked gratefully at Frank and then said, "I'm still wondering who was responsible for the attempts on Ted's life, though—and how much Don had to do with it."

"Don broke into Prescott's and also started the fire out there," the sheriff explained. "But Jessup was behind it all, with Mike Wood helping him out."

Sarah looked dumbfounded. "Brandon Jessup? Why?"

The sheriff continued. "Seems he's got grand plans to build a wild West theme park on the land he started buying up ten years ago, out by the Kingmaker. He didn't want the mining industry to start up right near his park."

"So that's why he wanted Ted Prescott out of the way."

"He tried to get someone else out of the way, too," Frank explained, gesturing to Toby. Sarah looked confused, and Frank went on.

"Toby Flint is really Jonas Middleton, the miner who was driven out of town, along with his fiancée, ten years ago. That's when Jessup first bought the land—Jessup's been looking for financial backing for his plan ever since."

Sarah again looked stunned. "I can't believe all that's happened in the name of greed," she said. "And to think I took part in it. I wish I could do something to turn this situation around."

"If you really want to make amends . . ." Joe began.

"Yes. Of course I do!" exclaimed Sarah eagerly.

"Ted Prescott had a good idea going for him, and he still does. Only he's spent all he'd saved and can't get started again on his own. Now, if he could find a partner with money . . ."

"Say no more, Joe," Sarah interrupted, smiling. She looked at Ted. "Well, Mr. Prescott, are you interested in resuming your work in the mine?"

Ted shrugged. "I'd like to get started again, but it will take plenty of money."

"If I financed you," Sarah said, "would you agree to a partnership?"

Ted thought briefly. "If you'd be willing to bring in a third partner, I'd do it."

"A third?" echoed Sarah, puzzled.

"How about it, Toby—that is, Jonas?" Ted asked. "Are you willing to take up your old profession and work with me?"

"Why not?" Toby answered with a big grin. "Beulah and I are both getting a little too old to wander around in that desert. You've got a deal."

"I own an old house that is unoccupied just now," said Sarah. "You can stay there for as long as you need to. My lawyers will work out the terms of the partnership, so that even if I have to go to jail for my part in what happened to you, you'll be properly funded."

"I expect you'll be given probation instead of jail time, Sarah," said the sheriff.

He turned to Frank and Joe. "I have a job I think you two could handle."

"Haven't we done enough for today?" Joe asked warily.

The sheriff laughed. "Well, yes you have. But tomorrow is the grand finale of Bonanza Days. This year we are re-creating a big shoot-out that took place here a hundred years ago. And we would like you guys to be sheriff and deputy."

Joe and Frank exchanged looks, and Calhoun quickly jumped in.

"Of course, we'll be using blank cartridges. But it'll be exciting. How about it?"

"If it's all the same to you, Sheriff," said Frank, "we're going up to Lake Tahoe with Callie and Kerry."

Both girls smiled and nodded in agreement.

"I guess we've done enough law-enforcing for a while," Joe said, with a deadpan expression. "Not that we don't appreciate the offer."

Frank and Joe's next case:

Bright Futures Development has announced the invention of a powerful new solar energy cell, and the Hardy boys have gone undercover to protect it from industrial spies. But the action proves too hot to handle: a company employee assigned to the solar cell lab has turned up dead!

Was it an inside job? Or was it a rival company out to burn the competition? Frank and Joe follow a trail of deceit and double-dealing and discover that the truth behind the solar power source is much darker than they suspected. Plenty of high-energy action awaits them as they fly straight into a fiery web of danger . . . in *Power Play*, Case #50 in The Hardy Boys Casefiles™.

SUPER HIGH TECH . . .
SUPER HIGH SPEED . . .
SUPER HIGH STAKES!

He's daring, he's resourceful, he's cool under fire. He's Tom Swift, the brilliant teen inventor racing toward the cutting edge of high-tech adventure. But Tom's latest invention—a high-flying, gravity-defying, superconductive skyboard—has fallen into the wrong hands. It has landed in the lair of the Black Dragon.

The Dragon, also known as Xavier Mace, is an elusive evil genius who means to turn Tom's toy into a weapon of world conquest! Swift will have to summon all his skill and cunning to thwart the madman. But the Black Dragon has devised a seemingly impenetrable defense system: he appears only as a laser-zapping hologram!

Turn the page for your very special preview of the first book in an exciting new series . . .

THE BLACK DRAGON

DON'T TELL ME I LOOK LIKE A GEEK," TOM Swift warned his friend Rick Cantwell. But he was grinning as he spoke into the microphone built into his crash helmet.

Tom knew he looked—well, weird. Besides the helmet that covered his blond hair, he was wearing heavy pads at his knees, elbows, and shoulders to protect his lean form. But weirdest of all were the heavy straps that bound his feet to an oversize surfboard, miles from any beach.

"I wouldn't say geek." Rick Cantwell's chuckle came clearly through Tom's earphones. "I'd say ner-r-r-r—"

His voice went into a stutter as Tom twisted a dial on the control panel at his waist. The surfboard under Tom's feet started humming loudly, then floated three feet off the ground.

Rick ran a hand through his sandy

brown hair, finally getting his voice back. "This is— I can't even say. It's like magic!"

"Not magic—electricity," Tom said, laughing. "Let's try it out."

He twisted a dial on the control panel. The humming grew louder, and the board sped up, skimming over the putty brown track on the ground. The track—a specially designed electromagnetic carpet—was just as important as the board. When the carpet powered up, it produced a giant electromagnetic field that "pushed" against the superconductive material in the skyboard, making it float.

"Okay, now," Tom said, turning up the dial. "Let's see how it moves."

The board picked up speed, riding on an invisible wave of magnetism. Tom bent forward a little, like a surfer playing a wave.

"It's like something out of a comic book. Look at that sucker go!" Rick yelled as Tom flashed past. "How fast can you push it?"

Tom shook his head.

"The problem with you, Rick, is you've got a reckless streak," Tom told him. "For you, there's only one setting worth trying—maximum. That's why *I'm* testing this board instead of you. You're a walking definition of the engineering term 'test to destruction.' "

"Yeah, but how fast does it go?" Rick asked.

Tom sighed. "*You'll* have to tell *me.* There's a radar gun—"

"Got it!" Rick said. "I'll just aim as you pass by and—" Rick's voice cut off with a loud gulp. "Um, would you believe seventy-five?"

Tom was crouched on the board now, looking as though he were fighting a strong wind—and he was. Air resistance of more than seventy miles an hour was trying to tug him off the board.

"This is serious," Rick said. "When do I get my turn?"

"Serious?" Tom started to laugh. "It sure is . . . so why am I having such a good time?"

"Hey, don't let your dad know." Rick was laughing, too.

"No, we'll just give him the facts and figures," Tom said. "Like how this thing climbs."

Using the left-hand dial to throttle back the speed, Tom turned the right-hand dial. "Yeeaaah!" he yelled as the board went screaming into the sky.

"Tom!" Rick shouted. "Are you okay?"

"Yeah." Tom's voice was a little shaky as he answered. "Make a note for Dad. This thing climbs like a jet plane."

The skyboard was making a lazy circle about a hundred feet in the air. Tom stared down. If he were a little higher, he could probably see Los Angeles. As it was, all of Central Hills was laid out at his feet.

Right below him, half-hidden in the hills, were the four square miles of Swift Enterprises. Tom could see the landing strips for planes and helicopters and the rocket launch site, but the center of his orbit was the testing field.

Tom noticed that the area was filling up with people. The technicians at Swift Enterprises were used to seeing strange things, but an eighteen-year-old on a surfboard with ten stories of thin air under him—that got attention.

Tom quickly brought the skyboard down to the ground, kicked free of the straps, and went over to Rick. "Let's set up the maneuverability test." He bent over the operations console, flicked a switch, and spoke into the microphone. "Robot! Do you hear me?"

"Receiving loud and clear." The robot sat in the center of the oval track, at a console that was a twin to the one Tom used. Around the robot a pattern of hatches was spread on the ground, making it look like a giant checkerboard.

"What are you supposed to be doing?" Rick's broad, good-natured face looked puzzled. "Playing chess?"

"Each square out there is a separate cell with a small but powerful electromagnet." Tom reached over to one side of the board and flicked some switches. "The trapdoors hide different, um, obstacles."

"What kind?" Rick asked.

Tom grinned. "Watch and see."

He hopped back on the skyboard, brought it to humming life, and took off. This time, instead of going around the test track, he swept across it onto the checkerboard. "When I reach you, robot, the test is over."

"Understood." The robot's hands flew across the control console.

Instantly, a hatch on the ground opened, and blasts of compressed air tried to blow Tom off the board. Tom sent the board into a zigzag, avoiding the blasts.

"Some test, Swift," Rick needled Tom over his headphones. "It looks more like a giant fun house."

A hatch directly in front of Tom opened, and a jet of water burst out of a huge squirt gun. Grabbing the control knobs at his waist, Tom sent the board hurtling out of the line of fire.

Hatches were opening up all around the checkerboard, sending a wild assortment of "weapons" at Tom. Bags of flour, squirts of paint, and even a barrage of cream pies went into the air. But Tom wove through the pattern of "fire" without being touched, like a hotdogger on an invisible wave.

'"You're almost there," Rick said excitedly.

Tom brought the board around for a landing behind the control console. The robot swiveled its head, its photocell eyes gleaming. Then its hand shot out to the power-grid controls, twisting a dial.

"Hey! You're not programmed to—"

That was as far as Tom got as the electromagnetic grid below him went crazy. The board bucked under his feet like an animal trying to toss him off.

Then it swooped into the air on a wild course, completely out of control. Tom struggled desperately, using the dials on his waist panel to try to straighten the skyboard.

He'd almost succeeded when a random magnetic blast first jerked the board, then sent it tumbling. Tom's feet were knocked right out of the foot straps.

Then he was falling, with nothing below him but seventy feet of thin air—and the hard, cold ground.

Tom threw out his arms like a skydiver, trying to slow his fall. "Rick—the air bags!" he yelled into his helmet mike.

Big white patches blossomed on the ground as Rick triggered the air bags. Then Tom's whole world turned white as he crashed into a mountain of inflated cushions.

That evening, at the beach, Tom unwrapped two skyboards—one red, one blue. Rick laid out the control panels and helmets and pads.

"You think of everything, Swift," he said, "even racing jackets." He held one up. "But couldn't you come up with something a little more stylish? Like black leather? This is kind of bulky, and it comes down below my hips."

"It's for safety, not fashion," Tom said. "There's a little ring up by the neck piece. If you get into any trouble on the board, yank it."

"And?" Rick said.

"And a dynasail comes out," Tom told him. "It fills with compressed air in about three seconds and is totally maneuverable. Rob put it together, based on some doodles I did."

Rick shook his head. "Let's hope we don't have to test *that*."

A crowd of kids came from the bonfires to marvel at the glowing track. Tom's sister, Sandra, came, too, carrying a plate heaped with hamburgers. "Some supplies for your trip," she said, a grin on her pretty face.

"Mmm, delicious." Rick grabbed another burger and started eating.

"How about you, Tom?" Mandy Coster asked.

"I'll have just one." Tom glanced at Rick. "Got to keep my racing weight down." He grinned as Rick nearly choked.

Pulling a cable he'd run from the van he used as a mobile lab, Tom hooked it up to the superconductor track he had sprayed on the sand. "We'll let it charge up while we get into our gear."

Rick slipped into the padding and jacket but stared at the helmet. "I can understand the mike and earphones, but I wouldn't think you'd need a tinted visor for night flying."

Tom grinned as he pulled on his own equipment. "Try it."

Rick put the helmet on. "I still don't see—" he began, slipping the visor down. "But I do now!"

Tom pulled down his visor—and the darkness around him disappeared. He could see everything clearly, but it looked like the landscape of another planet. The beach and the hills beyond were all tinted red, and the people around him glowed slightly. A brilliant band of color tinged the sky in the west, where the sun had set. The flame of the bonfire was blinding.

"Night vision!" Rick exclaimed.

"Ruby-lensed infrared visors," Tom said. "They actually read heat waves—the warmer the object, the brighter the light."

"Great. Well, I'm ready to go." Rick grabbed a board and headed for the track.

"This spray-on film isn't as strong as the other track," Tom warned. "We'll probably go up only a couple of feet—if we go up at all."

"Just one way to find out," Rick said, clamping his feet into the foot straps.

Tom tested the radio link with Rick and with his sister, who stood at the mobile lab's control board. "Sandra," he said into his mike, "everything ready?"

"Looks good from here," she said. "I'll move in with remote control if anything goes wrong."

"Okay, then." Tom clamped on his own straps. "Let's go for it!"

He and Rick moved the height controls. The boards floated into the air, bringing gasps from the kids. Tom could hear someone yell, "Outrageous!"

"How's it feel?" Tom asked Rick.

"A little wobbly," his friend replied.

"The spray must be a little uneven, so the magnetic field is uneven, too." Tom didn't mind the feeling. He felt as if he were bobbing on water. "Let's try once around the track," he said, "just to get the hang of it."

"Okay," Rick responded. "Then, when we come past Sandra, we'll speed it up."

His hand went to the speed control, and Tom followed. Their movement was more choppy than smooth, but they could handle it. Increasing the speed helped.

As they passed Sandra, Rick really poured it on. He whipped ahead of Tom, who sped up to pull even with him again.

"How about a little race?" Rick asked. Tom couldn't see Rick's face through the visor, but he knew his friend was grinning a challenge at him.

"Okay. But keep it under seventy—hey!"

Rick shot off again, with Tom zooming in pursuit. The slight roughness of the ride made the race more exciting. Instead of floating easily, Tom felt as if he were on the crest of a monster wave of energy, always on the brink of falling. The wind pulled at him as he upped his speed again.

Five feet ahead, Rick bent to cut his air resistance. Tom crouched a little lower, cutting his own wind profile. The clump of spectators passed in a blur.

"Hey, guys . . ." Sandra's voice cut in over their earphones. "We just clocked you doing ninety!"

Tom moved to slow down, but Rick just whooped and sped up. Then they were suddenly swooping up, gaining altitude at an incredible rate. "What the—?" Tom yelled, fighting his controls.

"You're not responding to remote control." Sandra's voice sounded scared.

"Tom—we've left the track!" Rick yelled. They still swept on, controlled by another magnetic field.

"Time to bail out," Tom said, tearing loose from the foot straps. He grabbed the ring on his jacket, pulled, and felt the dynasail fill and expand. He maneuvered it easily down to the beach.

But when he looked for Rick's dynasail, Tom saw him still crouched over his board. "Forget about it," Tom said. "Get off now!"

"I—I can't!" Rick's voice was tight. "My foot strap is stuck."

A tight, cold fist squeezed Tom's stomach as he watched his friend leave the magnetic field and start tumbling to the ground. "Rick!" he yelled.

A black shape came whispering out of

the sky. Through his infrared visor, Tom recognized the shape of an attack helicopter, painted and modified for a stealth mission.

The chopper dropped like a striking hawk for Rick and his board, a net flying out to catch them in midair.

As Tom stared, the dark intruder changed course, heading up and east while it drew his netted friend inside.

Inside the Black Dragon's complex, Tom saw swarms of worker robots turn, form ranks, and march off together. It was as if a single mind controlled them. Tom shivered. A single mind *did* control them—Xavier Mace. The disturbing question was, what did he intend to do with them?

Then, ahead of him and Rob—his seven-foot robot—he saw the small lab building that was their target.

Rob, back on the sensors, reported, "The entire place is surrounded by a high-energy electron field. And there are faint traces of a human presence inside the walls."

"Rick!" Tom said. "Well, the longer we wait, the more time we give the Black Dragon to get something unpleasant ready. Come on, Rob. We're going in."

In a moment, Tom stood outside the lab building, his duffel bag in hand and Rob by his side.

"Nothing's happening," Tom said as they walked toward the door. He pulled a little white disk out of his bag and stuffed it down the data slot. The locking mechanism went crazy, and the door slid half open.

A white-faced Rick Cantwell stood in the center of the room. His fists were clenched, and an ugly bruise stretched from his cheek to the line of his jaw. "I'm ready for you this time—"

His words cut off as he recognized the robot in the doorway. "Rob?" he said, the word mingling disbelief and delight. "Where's—?"

Tom lifted the visor on his helmet.

Rick's shoulders slumped in relief. "About time you came to get me." He started to grin, but it obviously hurt his face. "How'd you get in here without getting burned to a crisp? There's about ninety million volts of electricity outside."

"I don't have to worry about that in this suit," Tom said. "But you will." He reached into his bag of tricks. "We'll just have to—"

The huge screen on the wall flashed to life, revealing the face of the Black Dragon.

"Do I have the pleasure of talking to Tom Swift?" he asked.

"You do," Tom told him. "Though I don't know why it should please you."

"It's always a pleasure to talk to someone who invents an elegant solution to a difficult problem," Xavier Mace said with a smile. "In reverse engineering the samples of your skyboard that I obtained, I came to a lively appreciation of your genius. That's why I'm giving you this warning."

The face on the viewscreen leaned forward a little. "The secret of your superconductor is no longer a secret. Using the new technology, my automated work force is already producing a selection of attack robots."

Mace's smile became wider. "You have one minute to surrender, Tom Swift."